THE VELVET ROPE

ALSO BY BRENDA L. THOMAS

Fourplay: the dance of sensuality

Four Degrees of Heat
(with Crystal Lacey Winslow, Rochelle Alers,
& ReShonda Tate Billingsley)

THE
VELVET
ROPE

A NOVEL

BRENDA L. THOMAS

New York   London   Toronto   Sydney

An *Original* Publication of POCKET BOOKS

 DOWNTOWN PRESS, published by Pocket Books
1230 Avenue of the Americas
New York, NY 10020

Library of Congress Cataloging-in-Publication Data

Thomas, Brenda L., 1957-
　　The velvet rope : a novel / Brenda L. Thomas.—1st Downtown Press trade pbk. ed.
　　　p. cm.
　　ISBN 0-7434-7728-6
　　　1. African American businesspeople—Fiction. 2. African American women—Fiction.
　　3. Philadelphia (Pa.)—Fiction. 4. Businesswomen—Fiction. 5. Nightclubs—Fiction.
　　I. Title.

PS3620.H625V44 2005
813'.6—dc22

2004058260

First Downtown Press trade paperback edition January 2005

10　9　8　7　6　5　4　3　2　1

DOWNTOWN PRESS and colophon are
trademarks of Simon & Schuster, Inc.

Manufactured in the United States of America

For information regarding special discounts for bulk purchases,
please contact Simon & Schuster Special Sales at 1-800-456-6798
or business@simonandschuster.com.

Thurmond Thomas

To my Dad,
*   Keep on living 'cause when God made you, He broke*
the mold!

*   Love, Bones*

ACKNOWLEDGMENTS

All praises to Allah, most gracious, most merciful

This journey to my third novel has been a struggle and a blessing. The names of those who provided support is endless but certainly include many family members, friends, fans, book clubs, bookstores, reviewers, journalists, and fellow authors. I must give special thanks to my agent, Marc Gerald, who came on board right in the nick of time; to my editor, Selena James, who has proved to be a magician with the editing pen; and to Earl Cox, who continues to consult with me. Much appreciation goes to those who contributed feedback from reading early drafts: Phyllis Downey, Kim Gerald, Darryl Grant, Aisha Jordan-Moore, Leigh Karsch, and to so many folks who donated those great one-liners and allowed me to pick their brains.

Most importantly, I survive on the support—which continues to flow and hold me afloat when I doubt myself—from my daughter, Kelisha Rawlinson; my son-in-law, Maurice Carter; my son, Kelvin Rawlinson; and my beautiful granddaughters, Jazzlyn, Briana, and Jada, who are anxiously waiting to read my work. And never will I forget the men I stand on: my brothers, Joe, Gregory, and Jeffery, and the man who never leaves my side and with whom I spend all of my mornings, my father, Thurmond Thomas.

Some fantasies are best left unfulfilled.

—B. L. Thomas

PROLOGUE

TIFFANY L. JOHNSON
April

How could my life get any better? My family and closest friends were downstairs celebrating the groundbreaking of my new club, Teaz, which would be opening in less than five months. This venture had been a long time in the making. Now that the official renovation had begun, I was ready. I only had two months remaining before I left my PR position at Platinum Images. There was no more for me to learn about putting deals together or matching up clients with sponsors. I'd made thousands of dollars for clubs across the city, sometimes even tripling their business through my savvy promotions. Who knew, if this went well, I could open a club in New York, Miami, even L.A.

I walked down the hall toward the closet where I kept

clothes specifically for my nightlife. I knew exactly what I'd wear—black suede knee-high boots with three-inch heels and my short red suede dress.

My parents had always told me that I'd be at the helm of some business. I had always been good at being in charge. I had to be the leader in everything, probably because it made up for my insecurities. I always felt that people thought I was too beautiful to be smart. To compensate, I always made sure my intelligence shined as brightly as the strange beauty I'd been blessed with.

The first thing I planned to do after I resigned from my job was cut off this long black hair that hung down my back. I needed to look older, more cutting-edge for my new role as a nightclub owner.

Even though this nightclub venture occupied most of my time, the most important thing in my life was my man, Malik. I was happily engaged to a man I was actually in love with. Not bad for a girl who came from a family of adopted kids.

Hell, Malik was probably the only thing in my life that I wasn't in charge of. We usually met halfway on everything and if not, he would make the final decision and that was fine with me because he usually knew all the answers. Except about marriage and children. He'd been ready to get married right away and start working on a family. But I hadn't been ready. The idea of being a club owner had begun to appeal to me, and there was no way I was about to let marriage and a child get in the way. I had Malik, and he was all I needed. So, I turned my eye toward my career.

My goal? To reign as Philly's queen of the night.

MALIK D. SKINNER

I was so glad everyone was starting to leave the house. I'd promised my woman I would finish cleaning up while she got dressed. Tonight was important to her. It was also important to me because I wanted her new business, as well as our life together, to be a success.

Tiffany and I fell hard in love when we'd met four years ago. She was feisty and determined to be a successful publicist. Initially, she wasn't interested in a relationship and definitely not marriage, but I knew if I kept at it I could win her over. The first thing that attracted me to her was her beauty. It was sad to say, but a lot of the beautiful women I'd met over the years who'd looked good on my arm at company functions didn't hold a candle to Tiffany's beauty. And certainly not her drive. My woman was not only fine but smart.

Tiffany stood about five and a half feet tall. With her straight hair, slanted eyes, and velvety black skin, she constantly had men swarming around her. I often teased her about being jealous of all the men, but she'd never given me a reason not to trust her. It was more realistic that I was the one who couldn't be trusted. Women, especially white women at the law firm where I worked, were always coming on to me. I'd only slipped up once, on a business trip. It had been so tempting. Everybody had been drinking and mingling, and before I was aware of it, it was morning and I was waking up in someone else's bed. But since then I'd been faithful to Tiffany. I refused to go into the marriage being a cheat.

Tiffany was the perfect woman for me and I didn't intend to lose her. And Tiffany owning a club was about the best thing for my career. The crowd that followed her would certainly come in handy when it came time for me to run for office. Tiffany knew practically everyone in Philly, from both the wrong side and the right side of town. She was a take-charge type of woman, except when it came to something that involved me. At those times she could be flexible, and I was depending on that and her ability to keep a level head to get us through what was probably going to be our biggest hurdle—a secret I'd been keeping from her.

I stacked the dishes in the dishwasher and put out the recycle bin that was filled with liquor bottles from the night's party. Once the house was empty I'd get to work on the brief I had to write for work and draft some letters. Being a senior litigation associate at Covington, Myers & Levin was sometimes a nightmare. The payoff would be when I made partner. But before working tonight, I had to talk to Tiffany's sister, Kamille.

I wasn't looking forward to talking with Kamille, but I had to get it out of the way. Kamille had certainly never bothered me about it—she actually ignored me. But I knew it was a weight hanging over both of our heads. Though it might have taken place years ago, the results of our actions were threatening to be a devastating blow to all of our lives. If I wanted to keep my eyes on getting a political office in this city, I couldn't afford to have any dirt under my nails.

KAMILLE R. JOHNSON

I slipped into Tiffany's downstairs bathroom so I could do my thing. Tiffany would have killed me if she knew, but after tonight I wasn't going to do it anymore. It just made me feel so good. Almost like I could fly.

I was glad my parents had taken my boys home with them. I was hoping maybe I'd get lucky and be able to bring somebody home with me from the club later that night. That not having a steady man thing could be depressing, especially when the kids weren't around to annoy me.

Dumping the contents from my purse, I searched for the tiny pill that would give me the spark I needed for the night. There it was, in my makeup bag. I unwrapped it and sat it on the back of my tongue, chasing it with a paper cup of water.

Combing my fingers through my freshly bronzed hair, I admired my body in the mirror. I adjusted my bra so that more than enough cleavage was showing, then turned around to check myself out from behind. I rubbed my hands up and down my cocoa brown leather pants that fit my ass like saran wrap. My looks were sure to have all those girls at the club hating on me just because. Shit, it wasn't my fault that my skin was a creamy vanilla and I'd been blessed with thick, wavy, shoulder-length hair that wasn't sewn in. I had no idea where it came from. What I did know was that men loved me.

A little more lipstick and I was ready. All I had to do was sneak out before Malik caught up with me. He'd been leaving me messages, sounding all desperate. Twice tonight he'd attempted to talk to me. But there was nothing to talk about. It didn't matter. Didn't he know that you should just let sleeping dogs lie? Why was he even sweating it?

Someone was knocking on the bathroom door. . . . Malik. I could hear his ass trying to whisper.

"Kamille, are you in there? Kamille, open the door."

If he don't get off that damn door he'll spoil my high with his bullshit. I didn't get what Tiffany saw in his square ass anyway. I guessed she liked the fact that he was a lawyer. She'd always been about status and I'd always been about family. And when it came to men, I'd always been about me.

TIFFANY

I looked at Malik's picture on my side of the bed. His two-tone brown face was accentuated by a dark mustache and goatee. I loved that man, and there was no doubt in my mind that he loved me, too.

When I got downstairs I planned to tell Malik that my mother and I had picked a date for the wedding. A June bride, that's what I'd be. Nothing too extravagant. Maybe about one hundred people or so; neither one of us came from a big family.

I had a good network of people. Malik had been supporting me in my quest to open a nightclub even though I knew he'd rather I stayed in the public relations arena or maybe went for my master's degree. But I wanted my own business, something I could control.

Then there was my crazy sister, Kamille. If I could just get her to stop being so wild, maybe I could introduce her to someone really nice who would be accepting of her and her children. It hadn't been easy for her, raising three boys with three different fathers, but she'd done an excellent job. She'd been quite loose as a teenager, which was how she'd ended up with three sons by the time she was twenty-one. But our parents were always there for her, even though her life had turned out far different than they'd expected. She blamed all of her troubles on her biological parents, for whom she'd been searching since she was eighteen. Despite those wild teenage years, Kamille had done well for herself. She'd gotten her bachelor's degree and was working as an account manager at the Philadelphia Parking Authority.

Second to Kamille was my girl DJ Essence, who'd been rocking the turntables in clubs from Philly to Los Angeles. I'd met Essence a few years ago when I was handling the Clubs Across Philly event. I couldn't believe that a *white* female DJ could work the tables the way she did. When she went on break that night we'd shared a drink and she'd told me she'd been admiring me for a while. She'd noticed my style as I worked events around town and had been hoping to get the opportunity to work with me. From that night on we'd been hitting the clubs together. With her on board with Teaz there was no holding me back.

In the mirror I checked out my makeupless face and brushed my hair. I wished that I could wear more than lip gloss, but my skin was way too dark and I could never manage to apply the right shade of eye shadow on my chinky eyes.

I adjusted the belt on my dress, making sure it fit perfectly around my small waist. I was definitely not in a hurry to ruin my shape by having children. I wanted my breasts to sit up as long as possible and I surely didn't want my hips to spread. It would be great to go without a bra tonight, but Malik would have a fit.

Sitting down at my vanity, I took the time to carefully select my perfume for the night. Most women had a shoe fetish or a purse fetish; mine was for perfume, finding and selecting exquisite and rare fragrances. I never wanted to have the scent of another woman. I loved the crystal bottles and the way the stems felt when they touched my skin. The soft sensual floral fragrance of Quelques Fleurs would be my scent for tonight. Mmmmm, how could Malik ever resist me?

I was ready to go out, but I had to admit I was feeling a little horny. After working late last night, Malik had disappointed me by falling asleep just when I was ready for him. Before we'd moved in together we made love all the time—we couldn't get enough of each other. We'd both become so damn goal-oriented that sex had become an infrequent luxury.

Maybe I could get Malik to come up to give me a quickie. No, I had a better idea. I'd do what he told me should be my specialty. Yeah, that's what I'd do, give him something to think about while I was out for the night. Then, when I got back, maybe we could engage in something a little kinky.

Licking my lips, I realized that I was definitely going to have to add some more gloss.

MALIK

"Kamille, I know you're in there," I whispered against the closed door. "We need to talk."

No answer. Okay, I was getting paranoid. What if somebody else had gone into the bathroom? They'd be wondering why I was standing outside it, waiting for Tiffany's sister. But I was sure I'd seen her go into the bathroom, and everyone else had left. I planned to wait right there until she came out. Hopefully, Tiffany was still upstairs getting dressed. What the hell was Kamille doing in there?

I was just about to knock when I heard somebody coming, so I gave up and went back to the kitchen. It was empty except for the dog stretched out on the floor. I stepped over Bruiser's lazy ass and went back to cleaning up. Behind me I heard a door open, and when I turned around, sure enough, it was Kamille bouncing out of the bathroom. I knew she'd been in there, ignoring me. What the hell was she so happy about?

"Kamille, we need to talk."

"What the hell do you want?"

"You know what I want. We have to take care of this thing."

"Malik, are you crazy? Why would you want to dig up some old shit?"

"It's not so old that we can just forget it."

"Yeah, well, judging from that ring on my sister's finger, I consider the subject dead. Now, chill out."

TIFFANY

The living room was empty, so I assumed everyone had gone. Well, everyone but Kamille, that is, because we were riding to the club together. That's if she hadn't forgotten me. Malik was probably in the kitchen cleaning up. I doubted if my sister was helping him. Half the time I didn't think they liked each other. Kamille was probably just a little too wild for Malik, and he a little too rigid for her liking. He was forever complaining about how she didn't take care of her children properly. If it were up to Malik, every woman would be my clone.

Reaching inside the hall closet, I pulled out my short black raincoat and tossed it over the couch. I walked toward the kitchen, planning to whisper in Malik's ear what I wanted to do to him. I paused just outside the kitchen. I could hear strong words being exchanged between Malik and Kamille. I couldn't quite make out the specifics—their words were muffled. It almost sounded as if they were arguing. But why? And why was Bruiser growling? He never barked at Kamille and definitely not at Malik. Something was wrong. Then I heard Malik raise his voice.

"Damn it, Kamille. We're not gonna ignore this any longer. I have a lot at stake here and I don't want this hanging over my head."

I started to walk into the kitchen and ask what was hanging over my fiancé's head, but something told me that if I listened a bit longer, I'd find out.

"Look, Malik. Even if it *is* true, what can you do about it now? Just let the shit go."

"For starters, we're going to get tested. And depending on the results, we'll tell your sister."

"That's bullshit. I'm not subjecting Kareem to no fucking test. And you're damn sure not telling Tiffany."

My heart raced as I tried to imagine what they were keeping from me. I was too frozen in my spot to walk into the kitchen. Was something wrong with Kamille? My nephew? Was someone sick? And even worse, were Kamille and Malik having an affair? I held on to the bookcase for support as I continued to listen.

"Malik, if you tell her, you'll ruin everything. She's so happy with you and this club. You can't tell her, not right now. I'm begging you."

My sister was pleading and Kamille didn't do that.

"Kamille, you disgust me. Don't you want the best for your boys? This could work out."

"How? This is all about you, Malik. And what if he *is* yours? What do you want him to do, start calling you Daddy?"

My pulse quickened and I felt myself hyperventilating. I couldn't catch my breath, but I had to move, immediately, and find out what they were talking about. I burst into the kitchen.

"Malik, what the hell is going on? Please, please tell me you're not fucking my sister!" I begged, tripping over Bruiser as I made my way toward them. They didn't answer fast enough. They just stood there in shock. Without thinking, I snatched up the first thing within reach, the blender. Unable to remove the pitcher, I grabbed the entire thing, pulling the cord from the wall along with its switch plate. I threw it at Malik's head.

"Tiffany, what are you doing? Now, sit down so we can all talk," Malik shouted, ducking out of the way before the mixture of piña colada crashed against the refrigerator.

"I told you! I told you not to do this," Kamille screamed, her eyes wide with guilt as she covered her face with her hands.

"I don't wanna talk. I wanna know what's going on. Whose baby is whose, Kamille?" I said, fighting the urge to cry at their betrayal.

"Sis, it's not like that. It was a long time ago." My sister's eyes brimmed with tears. She was always so emotional and weak. It took nothing to make her cry.

"You bitch. Get out of my house before I kill you!" I screamed at her, too furious to listen to her explanations.

Kamille wasn't moving fast enough, so I looked around the kitchen for another missile. This time I picked up an open jar of Hellmann's mayonnaise and hurled it in her direction. It slammed into the microwave before landing in Bruiser's bowl. The dog scurried out of the way.

"Tiffany, just listen, damn it, before you go crazy," Malik pleaded.

"Hell no! You get the fuck out, too."

Scooping up the bowl of my brother's homemade barbeque sauce, I tossed it Malik's way. The bowl hit the floor, but not before the red sauce splashed and ran down the front of Malik's favorite cashmere sweater. By now I was aiming anything I could get my hands on in their direction, including a bowl of pasta salad that broke the clock over the kitchen doorway.

"Please, sis, listen to Malik."

I looked at her as my hand reached for the pineapple that

lay half sliced on the cutting board. I threw that, hitting my sister on the shoulder.

Bruiser was barking frantically, jumping up on me, helping to turn the scene into a chaos-filled nightmare. Kamille tried to run out of the kitchen, but I grabbed a handful of her hair, spinning her around to face me.

"You low-life bitch. You'll sleep with anybody, won't you?" I said, spitting my words in her face.

Malik grabbed me from behind by the shoulders, pulling me away from Kamille. She wiggled out of my grip and ran crying from the house. I ran after her, picking up our Blues Man statue on my way out the front door. Just as she closed the door to her car, I threw the statue, creating a huge dent in the hood of her black Maxima.

Next it was Malik's turn. I strode back into the kitchen, where he was picking up the broken glass. I was going to kill him.

"You bastard!"

"Damn it, Tiffany. Will you just sit down and listen so you'll understand what—"

"Understand this, motha . . ." I said, lunging at him with a pair of scissors I'd grabbed from the utility rack.

He backed up against the basement door. "You're going to hurt somebody. Calm down."

"I'm not calming down until you get out my face. I hate you, Malik. How could you do this to me?" Instead of moving out of my way, he tried to grab my wrists and take the scissors from my hand. I wrestled with him, continuing to jab at him with the scissors until I cut into the sleeve of his sweater.

He pulled away from me and grabbed hold of his arm to stop the blood that came leaking out. He headed for the door but I was still not satisfied. I looked around for another way to hurt him.

"Tiffany, you've lost your damn mind!"

"Get out! Get out, you bastard!" I yelled, throwing the plant that sat on the windowsill over the sink. But he was already gone.

I rushed to the living room and slammed the door behind him. Bruiser looked at me, whining.

"What the fuck are you looking at?"

My eyes swept across the neat little living room that Malik and I had furnished. All I could think about was destroying it. I went around and threw every piece of framed art onto the floor, along with the statues and masks we'd collected. Within minutes the downstairs was in shambles, but I was still full of rage. I went upstairs to the second floor, which we'd recently renovated. I knocked over lamps, swept all the bottles of cologne from Malik's dresser, and then moved on to my vanity. Without the least bit of hesitation, I used a wooden hanger to knock all my hard-found fragrances to the floor. If I'd had matches I would've set the entire place on fire. My gaze moved to the phone when it started ringing, the sound drilling into my head. So I went through the house and, one by one, I yanked the phones from the sockets.

When I'd exhausted myself and there was nothing left to destroy, I went back into the kitchen and found an unbroken bottle of Belvedere. I removed the cap, slumped into a chair, and gulped down its fiery contents.

1

HANGOVER

It was almost noon when I found myself hanging off the living room couch. I wanted to sleep until Malik woke me and told me I'd had a nightmare. But when I looked around the ravaged room, I knew I hadn't been dreaming. The reality was that I'd found out my fiancé and my sister had had a child together.

I tried to sit up, but my entire body was too heavy to move. I squeezed my eyes shut, but my head hurt too bad to let me resume sleeping. With much effort I managed to drag myself upstairs. I screamed when I saw all my prized perfume bottles broken and empty on the bedroom floor.

I went into the bathroom and stepped into the shower stall, not even realizing until I turned on the water that I was fully dressed in my clothes from the previous night. I peeled off the ruined suede boots, stepped out of my stockings and my soggy suede dress, and tossed them toward the trash can. I turned the knob and ran the water as hot as I could and when my skin began to burn I turned it to warm. Sliding down into the tub, I cried until the icy water drove me out.

I found Bruiser panting at the bathroom door, begging to go outside. So I put on my robe and returned downstairs to the kitchen. Broken dishes lying among puddles of barbeque sauce and mayonnaise. . . . Malik's cell phone floating in the dishpan. . . . My God, I'd lost my mind! But didn't I have the right?

Why had Malik and Kamille done this to me? I tried to recall what they'd said, which only caused my head to start spinning. I held on to the kitchen sink to steady the pain that had started to dig a hole in my belly. I screamed out to the empty kitchen, "Please, tell me this isn't happening. Malik, why'd you do this?" My sobs racked my entire body. I looked around for somewhere to hurl the pain, but everything was already destroyed.

Gradually I realized someone was banging on the front door. I tried to ignore it, but the person was persistent, first pounding with the knocker and then ringing the bell. Surely Malik or Kamille didn't have the nerve to return. I kicked the overturned plants out my way and peered through the peephole. Essence. I pulled open the door and saw that her expression reflected what I was feeling. It hadn't been a nightmare. I sunk into her arms, sobbing.

"Baby, I'm so sorry."

"Essence, please tell me why this is happening."

She sat me on the couch and tried to soothe my cries. Her sympathy only made it hurt worse.

"It'll work out."

"How can you say that?" I asked, looking up at her, hoping that it could.

She searched for a tissue to wipe the tears and mucus that ran down my chin, all the while trying not to gawk at the ravaged house that had always been kept neat.

"I spoke to Kamille," she said softly, as if my sister's name might ignite a fury in me.

Falling back onto the couch, I told her, "I don't wanna hear nothing they have to say. You hear me?"

"Tiff, just listen, okay. Kamille called me last night, and she really feels bad about all this. You gotta realize this happened a long time ago."

"It doesn't matter when it happened. Don't you understand? Malik is my nephew's father. He slept with my damn sister, Essence."

"You can't be so sure of that. At least not yet. Malik told me they plan to get a DNA test."

"He called you, too?"

"No, he came to see me last night at El Vez."

"For what?" I asked, knowing that Malik didn't do the club scene unless he was accompanying me.

"Malik loves you, Tiffany. You know that. He's devastated that you found out this way."

"Are you crazy? I can't believe you're taking up for them. They betrayed me, Essence." I sat there shaking my head and crying while Essence rubbed my back.

"Listen, sweetheart. You know what? You're right, they did keep a terrible secret from you, but you can't let it destroy you and you damn well better remember that we have a club to open. You know you're gonna have to talk to them at some point."

"Look, Essence. This is too much for me to think about right now. The club, them, my nephew. Let's just talk about this later, okay? Now, go on and get out of here so I can try to get myself together."

"You sure you don't want me to help you clean up?" she asked, picking up an overturned lamp. "What about a cup of coffee?"

"No, I'll be fine," I lied, ignoring the debris and opening the front door for her.

But when she left all I could do was lie on the couch crying. I knew I was far from fine and seriously doubted if anything in my life would ever be right again.

After I'd wrung myself dry of the seemingly endless tears, I managed to get dressed. By habit I got in my truck and drove around the corner to the Coffee Room Café at Twenty-sixth and Pennsylvania Avenue. It was where Malik and I went every Saturday morning for breakfast.

I wasn't in the mood for chatting with the familiar waitress, and she got the message when I mumbled my order and refused to look at her. I needed to make sense of what had happened in the last twenty-four hours. I popped two Tylenol and chased them with coffee, scalding the roof of my mouth trying to drink the liquid too hastily.

I thought about my younger sister. We were best friends

and probably as close as sisters could get. We confided everything in each other, yet she'd held back about her relationship with Malik. As I stared out the window onto East River Drive, I just couldn't fathom how Malik had become Kareem's father. Kamille had told my parents and me that the young man who'd fathered Kareem when my sister was seventeen had gone to jail right before Kareem was born. She'd only been seeing him for a few months before she became pregnant. And whenever I'd asked about Kareem's father, she said he was still incarcerated.

But who knew, maybe there never was another man. Maybe that had just been a story she and Malik had concocted so as not to ruin his budding career and now our relationship.

And Malik, as far as I knew, had never cheated on me. If he had, he'd been damn good at it. I used to believe he loved me, but maybe he didn't. Right now I didn't know the answer to anything.

My racing thoughts were making me crazy, as was my ringing cell phone. I looked at the number. It was Malik calling me from his car. There was no way I was answering it.

I was just about to leave when I noticed a black Lincoln Town Car bearing municipal tags conveniently parking in a no-parking zone. I prayed it wasn't anyone we knew. When the driver's door swung open I saw that it was G-dog. Damn it, he was a pain in my ass.

Gregory D. Haney III, also known as G-dog, was a patron of every club in the city, so needless to say our paths crossed on a regular basis. To make matters worse, he never missed the opportunity to flirt with me. To add to his self-importance, he boasted he was the biracial son of Philadelphia's powerful new district attorney. I'd seen his father on TV several times. A sharp dresser with striking features, he was known as a ladies' man, and his son liked to think he was, too.

I kept my eyes on G-dog as he strolled through the door. I tried to figure out a way to slip out of there without being seen. For the first time I noticed that he wasn't particularly tall, barely six feet and kind of squatty, but handsome nonetheless, with his high-yella complexion and short curly hair. At the clubs he always wore a baseball cap and jeans, but now that he was probably coming from his job at the Department of Recreation, he wore a button-down sweater, khakis, and a brown leather jacket.

After a few moments I realized there was no way I was going to get out of the café without him seeing me. While he stood talking with the cashier, I pushed my chair back and was about to get up when he smiled and made his way to my table.

"What's up, Tiff? You look like you had a rough night," he commented, pulling out a chair to sit down across from me.

Damn, I'd forgotten to bring my sunglasses to cover my swollen eyes. I lowered my head. I was sure I looked like hell.

Coughing to clear my throat, I said, "What's up, G-dog? I was just about to get outta here."

"You don't have to brush me off. I just wanted to say congratulations on the club," he said, reaching across the table to shake my hand.

"Oh, uh, thanks."

My hands were shaking and my eyes were welling up. I used the back of my hand to wipe the tears away, hoping G-dog hadn't noticed.

"Safe to assume that nigga Malik been treating you well?" he asked, looking down at the two-carat diamond ring I wore.

Malik was well known in Philadelphia as a rising star because of his fast-growing legal and political career. He'd been praised in the *Legal Intelligencer* for his battle with the DA's office when they'd wrongly accused one of Malik's clients of the Fenton Street murders. Malik had gotten the case overturned, so he was far from being a friend of the district attorney.

My mind drifted as I remembered how Malik had surprised me with dinner at McCormick and Schmick's to celebrate with him. Before I knew it, tears fell onto my cheeks.

"Yo, what's up? What's wrong?" G-dog asked, lifting up my chin with his hand.

I shook his hand off. "I'm fine."

"Well, a brother can see that's a touchy subject. Anyway, even though you didn't invite me to your groundbreaking, I'd still like to lend you my assistance with anything you need from me or my father's office." He placed his business card in my hand.

Didn't he realize yet that I wanted nothing to do with him?

My cell phone rang again, this time in unison with G-dog's cell phone. I refused to answer, but while he answered his call I scrolled through my list of missed calls: Kamille, twice; Essence, once; Malik, three times from his office at Covington, Myers & Levin, and twice from his car.

G-dog hung up and said, "Well?" He pointed at his business card laying in front of me.

"I don't think I'll be needing you or your father for anything," I answered, as my fingers rapidly tapped against my coffee mug.

"I wouldn't be too sure of that. Looks to me, by those swollen eyes, that you don't know what you need."

I didn't want the pain I was in to be that obvious. There had to be some way for me to get this under control. I didn't want to put my professional future in jeopardy.

I snatched my purse off the back of my chair and said, "Go to hell, G-dog," and walked out of the restaurant.

After driving back to the house, I went upstairs and lay across the bed trying to make sense out of how I'd lost control of my life. Up until now everything had gone as I'd planned it. How could I not have known about Malik and Kamille? There had to have been a sign, some passing affection. This was not the love I'd planned for. Love, at least my love with Malik, was not supposed to hurt. The relationships I'd had in the past had been meaningless and never affected me like this when they ended. Malik and I had been perfect, but now he was no better than all the other losers I'd dated before him.

Two hours later I woke up to Bruiser's barking outside my window. When I walked to the top of the stairs, I found Malik standing at the bottom.

"What do you want?" I asked, too exhausted to fight with him.

"Tiffany, we need to talk. Why haven't you returned my calls?"

I laughed. "You gotta be kidding."

I walked down the stairs to let Bruiser in the house, but rather than let me pass, Malik held on to my arm.

"Tiffany, your sister and I are getting a blood test to settle this thing."

"You and my sister deceived me from the time I met you. Even if you're not Kareem's father, do you think that I'd still want to be in a relationship with you?"

"Tiffany, I love you. I don't want your sister or anything that comes with her. The first time you introduced me to your sister I didn't even remember who the hell she was."

"You're saying you're not going to play daddy? Then I guess you are the piece of shit I thought you were."

"Woman, don't you understand? If I can't have you, then I don't want anything to do with your sister or your nephew."

His cruel words were painful and confusing. How could he talk so harshly about Kamille and the child he'd fathered? Tears began to roll down my cheeks before I could swallow them to speak.

"Tiffany, I'm sorry. I didn't mean that. You know I'd take care of any child that belongs to me. But I can't let you go. I love you. I swear I won't let you go."

He tried to hug me, but when I stood stiff in his arms he dropped them and lowered his head. He was hurting, too, but he deserved it. I could tell by his swollen and red eyes that he hadn't slept and that he'd probably been crying.

"Malik."

He looked up, hopeful.

"I want you out of my house and out of my life."

"You're going about this all wrong, Tiffany. You're not even giving me a chance to explain. This isn't like you, reacting like this. Please don't do this to us."

"Really? You have me so figured out. So damn methodical, am I? Well, that's over."

"I can't deal with you when you're not making sense," he said, then walked out the front door.

I wanted to run after him and scream and yell until the pain went away, but I didn't want my nosy neighbors to think I was crazy. Once his car was gone I tried to put the house back in some order, but my efforts seemed useless. After a few moments my cell phone rang. I saw my sister's number come up, so I hit DECLINE. She called again. On the third ring I snatched up the phone.

"Leave me alone, Kamille. I don't want shit to do with you! You're a dirty whore," I screamed into the mouthpiece.

"Tiffany, what is going on? Malik told me you tore up the house."

It was my mother.

"Mom, don't get in the middle of this. You have no idea what's going on."

"You're talking crazy. Are you on drugs? Your sister wants to talk to you."

"Tell my sister to kiss my ass!"

"Don't you use those words with me, Tiffany Johnson. I didn't—"

Click. I hung up.

I'd had enough of everybody's input. It was Saturday night and I needed to get out of the house and go someplace where I wouldn't be noticed and wouldn't have to talk about business or my personal life. If I didn't get out of the house, I would explode.

I phoned Essence, and when she told me what club she was at I frantically drove down the expressway to South Philly to join her. She was easy to spot in one of her signature fedora hats, sitting at a table at the Pousse Café. As usual, Essence was surrounded by women, bopping her head to the sounds of Beyoncé belting out "Dangerously in Love." She reveled in being the center of attention, so dee-jaying was the perfect job for her. Essence was probably the only white female DJ with such a large black following. Just like male DJs who picked up women, Essence had the pleasure of picking up both men and women. When she was on the turntables, all eyes were on her and nobody saw color.

Her groupies dispersed when I walked up and slid into the booth.

"Damn, girl, you look bad," she stated, looking me over before hugging me.

"Malik came back to the house tonight."

"Good. Did you talk with him?"

"I asked him to move out. What are you drinking?" I asked, sipping from her glass.

"Tiff, you're moving too fast. Don't you want to wait till the tests come back?"

The waitress came over and took our drink orders.

"What is it with everybody? I'm not the one who was out fucking around."

"I'm sorry. I didn't mean to upset you. It's just that I don't want everything to be ruined."

"I'm not letting them ruin anything. I'll get through this. Hell, maybe I'll find me somebody to sleep with," I said, as I surveyed the room filled with gay women.

"That's bullshit. Not on my watch."

The waitress reappeared with our drinks. I held my glass up to hers and for the next hour we drank shots of tequila.

By 11:00 P.M. I'd managed to get wasted and was ready to join in the fun everyone else seemed to be having. For the first time I was aware of the variety of women available when you're in a club where it's always ladies' night. These women were sensual and totally uninhibited in the way they danced. I could clearly see why Essence boasted that she loved men, yet craved women. And right now I craved them, too.

Essence left me to go dance with a curvaceous woman I'd seen her with before. After I sat alone nursing my drink, a sister asked me to dance, so I sashayed my black and half-drunk ass onto the small dance floor. I was having such a good time that after three songs I'd actually forgotten about my broken heart. And that's when a woman who'd been eyeing me stepped in between me and the sister I'd been dancing with. I was so sweaty and drunk that I had to lean against her to stay on my feet.

"This your first time here, sexy?"

"Nope," I answered, as I turned around in search of

Essence. I spotted her onstage with three women vying for her attention.

"You wanna get down?" she asked in my ear over the loud music.

"Sure, whatever." I'd always wondered what foreplay with a woman was like.

She grabbed my hand and I followed her into the ladies' room. She opened the door to one of the stalls and we squeezed inside.

"Damn, you're black, but you're fine as hell," she said, running her hands over my hips.

I couldn't count the many times I'd heard that line. I wanted to tell her she was the one who was sexy, with her pierced belly button and tank top that read LUCKY across the front.

I moved closer, gyrating my body against hers.

"I'd sure like to get in those panties tonight," she said, as if she were a man seducing me. Her throaty voice made it sound even more enticing.

With her hot breath against my ear, she asked, "What's your name, Black Angel?"

If she didn't already know who I was, I wasn't about to tell her. In order to stop her questions I pressed my lips against her open mouth, then pulled away, surprised at my own aggressiveness.

"Shit, I can see I got me a little hottie tonight, eh? We gonna have some fun."

I kissed her again, but this time she clasped her hands around the back of my neck and moved her tongue around my mouth until I didn't want to pull away.

"You here with anybody?" she asked.

"Just you and me. Isn't that enough?" I answered, before placing my hand over her breast and squeezing it.

"Not too rough, honey. Here, this will make it easier for you," she said, lifting her shirt and gently placing my hand on her naked breast.

"Go ahead, suck Mommy's titties," she said, pushing her breast toward me.

I hesitated at first, but then bent my head and flicked my tongue around her pink areola. It was so soft and spongy that I opened my mouth and took in as much as I could. I almost wanted to laugh because it felt like I was sucking on a marshmallow.

"Girl, you're good. Now, here, take a little of this."

I let her wet breast slide out of my mouth and held my head up to see what she was giving me. Under her fingernail was some white powder. She dabbed it onto my tongue, numbing it. I assumed it was cocaine.

With her hands in my hair, she lifted my face to hers and stuck her tongue deep in my mouth. The only thing different from kissing a man was that there was no mustache to tickle my lips or beard stubble to scratch my face. I wondered what other parts of her body might be soft where a man's were hard. She must've known what I was thinking, because she put her hand under my skirt in search of my thong. I followed her lead by putting my hands between her legs in that hot spot in the fold of her jeans.

I was so wrapped up with my own desire to get lost that I paid no attention to the noise from the club when the bathroom door opened. That is, until I heard Essence talking on the other side of the stall door.

"Just stay still. Won't nobody know you're in here," the woman said, her fingers reaching that tender spot right beneath the opening of my vagina.

"Tiffany, I saw you come in here. Now, I'm giving you one minute to get out here before I kick the frickin' door in."

"Fuck her, baby, you gotta do you."

I looked at the woman, who probably could've brought me to climax. She was clearly annoyed that we had been interrupted.

"Leave her alone," she shouted back to Essence.

But she had no idea what a crazy white girl Essence was, so rather than cause a fight I pulled away and unlocked the stall door.

"What do *you* want?" the woman asked from behind me.

"Bitch, are you crazy, messing with my people? If I see you near her again I will kick your ass," Essence warned, knocking the bag of coke from her hand.

The woman immediately backed down.

I tried to defend myself. "Essence, you can't tell me what to do. I'm a grown woman."

"Well, check this out. I'm taking your grown ass home. Now, let's go," she demanded, yanking me out of the stall.

Once we were in my truck I begged her not to take me back to my house in Brewery Town. She agreed, and instead drove me to her home in University City. When we got inside her apartment I went to the refrigerator to look for something to drink, then followed her to her bedroom.

"Tiffany, listen, I know you're hurting, but you can't go around acting like this, drinking and making out with dykes and shit. It's not going to change anything. I mean, it's just not your M.O. Pretty soon you're gonna have to talk to Malik and Kamille."

"Aww, shut up. Don't nobody know how I feel," I said, watching as she undressed, still wondering what it would feel like to have sex with a woman. "Make love to me, Essence."

"Bitch, you're drunk. You don't know what you're talking about. Take your ass in the other room and go to bed."

"I don't care what you say, somebody will make love to me tonight."

"Go to sleep," she said, and climbed into bed.

As soon as I lay across the bed in her guest room, thoughts of Malik and Kamille started racing through my head and killing my tequila high. Maybe he liked my sister better than me. Maybe her lovemaking was able to keep him awake at night. My sister was always bragging about how good she could work her body during sex, that she could make a man whimper. Had Malik been one of those men?

I knew then who I'd call. I searched through my purse for the card he'd given me.

"Yeah, it's Tiffany."

"Oh shit, how'd I get lucky to get this late-night booty call?" G-dog asked.

"Does it matter?"

"Not to me. Why don't you come up the way? You know where I'm at."

Before driving out to Nights Over Broadway, a raunchy strip club where most of the brothers hung out after 3:00 A.M., I drove past my house to see if there was any sign of Malik. The place was dark and I felt bad that I hadn't been home to let Bruiser out. I was about to get out of my truck when I saw Malik's Volvo come from around the opposite corner. I watched as he parked outside our house. He went in, then came back outside, taking an overexcited Bruiser for a walk. I watched as he answered his cell phone, smiling at whoever the caller was. Who would be calling him at three o'clock in the morning? I became infuriated when I thought that maybe it was my sister. Maybe they were making plans. I started my engine and raced off to meet G-dog.

Twenty minutes later, when I walked into the crowded and smoky after-hours spot, all eyes turned to me. It was a place that I didn't frequent, but being in this business you had to know them all. I spoke to those who spoke to me, and paid no attention to the envious women who rolled their eyes.

G-dog was standing at the far end of the bar engaged in conversation both on his cell phone and with a brother standing next to him. I wasn't even sure how he could hear with the loud rap music that crackled out of the speakers.

"Tell her what you drinking," he said, nodding toward the topless barmaid.

"Absolut and cranberry," I said, watching the overworked and naked strippers trying to earn tips. This strip club was far from a gentleman's club. It was one of those places where anything goes.

"Pretty strong drink. So what you been up to this time of morning?" he asked, after disconnecting his call.

"Hanging out with Essence."

Laughing, he said, "I didn't know you was into that."

"G-dog, it's a whole lot you don't know about Tiffany Johnson."

"Damn, girl, all this time I thought you was a straight-up businesswoman, but now you showing me some different shit."

He was right. I'd been totally out of character since Malik and Kamille's secret had been exposed. And for the first time I'd stopped caring what people thought about me and what I thought about myself. All I wanted was for the pain to disappear. Maybe G-dog could make that happen. I'd always prided myself on the fact that I hadn't been with another man since I'd met Malik. I'd never had a reason to seek love or sex elsewhere, but now maybe I did. Maybe that's just what I needed.

"Why are you always telling me you want a piece of Teaz?" I asked him as he downed a glass of Hypnotic.

"I want a piece alright," he mumbled, and then said louder, "Shit, I been trying to get in on anything you were a part of for a long time. Your uppity ass just been ignoring me. But I guess you finally realize that nothing goes down in Philly that I'm not part of."

"I'm supposed to believe you're that powerful?"

"Well, if I ain't, my daddy sure is."

I reached over, fingered the gold hoop in his right ear, and said, "So, what part of Tiffany do you want?"

He eyed me up and down, then kissed me on the lips. "All I can get," he answered.

The sun was coming up when we left the club and I staggered to G-dog's truck. I was sure I'd never been that drunk before in my life. When we arrived at my house I handed him my purse to find my keys. He unlocked the door but backed away when a growling Bruiser met us. I tried to tell him that Bruiser wouldn't bite, but he waited until I put the dog in the backyard before he would come in.

Heading toward the kitchen, I stammered, "You want a drink?"

"You've had enough of that shit," he answered, observing my living space.

I turned around and got up close enough to him to feel his hard dick against my thigh.

Holding on to the waist of his pants, I said, "Let's go upstairs, G."

"I don't think you wanna do this. What if your nigga comes home?" he asked, looking around as if Malik was going to pop out of the other room.

"My so-called *nigga* don't live here no more," I said, trying to kiss him while he talked.

"Girl, I ain't trying to get shot."

"Aww, c'mon, G-dog. You mean you don't want to make love to me with this?" I asked, grabbing a handful of his hardness.

He wasted no time responding to my touch. He kissed me hard, swallowing my tongue in his mouth while his hands unzipped the front of my sweater.

"Girl, I been waiting to get this," he exclaimed, bending over to trail kisses along my stomach.

The house phone began to ring, but I ignored it, figuring it was probably Essence checking to see if I was home. I stepped out of my skirt, then pulled G-dog's shirt over his head and returned to his arms. The phone rang again. Whoever it was must've been hitting redial, determined to reach me.

"You better answer that. Somebody trying to get at you."

I walked over to the phone and checked the caller ID. It was Malik. Fuck him. But it was too late. His interruption had changed the mood.

"That was him, wasn't it?"

I shrugged.

"Maybe we should chill out. I can't afford to have no problems."

"G-dog, I don't care about him. I need this really bad."

"Tiffany, that man ain't crazy. How 'bout you go upstairs to bed?"

"Why the hell is everybody telling me to go to sleep? I been asleep for the last few years while people been fucking behind my back."

"Hey, check this out. I don't know what that's all about, but I'm putting your ass to bed." In one swift move he lifted me off my feet and carried me upstairs.

It was after twelve o'clock on Sunday when G-dog showed up in my bedroom doorway. I couldn't quite remember what had happened the night before, but if he was here bringing me coffee, then I was too embarrassed to find out.

When he sat on the end of my bed my head started spinning and my stomach began to churn, a feeling I hadn't had since college. I ran into the bathroom and kneeled in front of the toilet, where I stayed until G-dog cleaned me up and carried me back to bed.

"Damn, girl, you don't need to drink. Here, sip this shit," he said, handing me a cup of Dunkin' Donuts coffee. He applied a wet towel to my face, which felt warm and soothing. "I had your truck brought down from the club this morning," he said.

"Thanks. I still can't believe I drank all that stuff. I hope I didn't do anything stupid," I said, before sipping the steaming black coffee.

"Not exactly, but if that nigga hadn't called, you would've gotten what you were asking for."

"You're kidding, right? I was asking you to . . ."

He nodded and chuckled.

"I am so sorry. I shouldn't have dragged you into this. I hope you can forgive me."

"Why don't you tell me what's up first?"

On a whim I did something I didn't usually do, and that was talk to people about my personal affairs. He'd already seen me at my worst, which made it a little easier to be vulnerable with him. I mean, he'd had the perfect opportunity to take advantage of me but had only acted like a real gentleman, which led me to believe that maybe G-dog wasn't so bad after all. So I told him the entire story about Malik and Kamille, that is, as much as I knew. Somehow I was able to get through it without crying.

"And last night was to get back at him?"

"G-dog, I don't know what it was. I was just trying to get through the pain. I'm sorry if you thought I was using you, and I'm sorry about the way I treated you at the café."

He took his time to think about his answer, kissed me on the forehead, and then said, "Hey, it's cool. For you, girl, I'll ride the bench. Plus, you don't have anything to be sorry about. I mean, that nigga did some foul shit. But enough of that. Check this out. I have to go down to the Keys this evening to handle some real estate business. You wanna go with me?"

"Florida? Today?"

"Sure. What else you got going?"

"I can't. I have to work through some stuff. But I appreciate the invitation."

He stood up to leave. "You sure you gonna be okay by yourself?"

"I don't have a choice."

2

SLEIGHT OF HAND

I managed to drag myself into work on Monday morning with no idea of how I would get through the day. The first person to come into my office was my assistant, Kendra. How is it that people always know when you're having man problems, especially other women? We must give off a certain look or vibe that can't be confused with any other kind of pain.

"Bad weekend with Malik, boss?"

"Please, today's not a good day, Kendra."

"I can see that," she mumbled under her breath. "I doubt if you care, but Malik's on the phone for you and has been burning up the lines all morning. I assume you don't want to talk to him."

"Put him in voice mail and close my door on your way out."

I looked at my calendar. It was full this week because I was covering for Michael, the firm's lead partner, who was on vacation. I had no idea how I would handle his accounts and mine, but maybe staying busy would help keep my thoughts about Malik at bay.

I went to the conference room for a meeting to put the final touches on the upcoming NAACP convention. Then to a meeting with the riverfront committee about the Panache Hotel and Casino, which would be breaking ground next fall. And just before noon I had a conference call with Convention Center management, who didn't want to give me a break on pricing for the upcoming Narcotics Anonymous convention. But even with all these meetings, my mind kept drifting back to Malik.

From what I'd learned through Essence, Malik and Kamille had supposedly met at a party in Philly while he was home on break from Harvard Law. He'd taken her back to his apartment in New Jersey, where they'd spent the weekend and, possibly, conceived my nephew Kareem. Supposedly, that was the extent of their relationship. It was only when Malik took my nephews home one day that he realized that Kamille was the woman he'd spent the weekend with. And, according to Essence, they'd yet to make arrangements to take the blood test, which only proved to me that they were already convinced that Malik was Kareem's father.

When I'd met Malik four years ago he'd just started work-

ing at Covington and our agency had been hired to help
them with a celebrity client. I'd noticed him immediately, as
he was one of the few clean-shaven, well-dressed black men.
When he'd tried to flirt with me, I'd teased him about his
being too young for me. But hell, I was only about twenty-
three. I was surprised when he'd kindly informed me that he
was actually three years my senior.

We'd exchanged business cards, and later that evening
when I'd checked my voice mail at work, he'd already left
me a message. I waited two days before returning his call to
the house where he lived with his grandmother. That same
night we met at the Breakfast Klub restaurant for a late
dinner.

Malik and I dated for about two months before I introduced him to my family. I clearly remember the day he met
Kamille—and there'd been no look of recognition on either
of their faces. They'd actually gotten along rather well until
the night Malik had taken my nephews to Kamille's house
after they'd spent the weekend with us. When he came back
that night he was in a sour mood, and when I'd asked him
what was wrong he'd said that my sister was sitting in her
house smoking weed when he'd dropped off the kids. I
should've suspected something then, especially when he said
he had a lot of work to do and needed to go home. Shortly
after that he suggested we move in together, and from that
point on Malik and Kamille always seemed to rub each other
the wrong way. I'd just brushed it all off as personality differ-
ences.

After lunch I pushed paper around my desk, trying to

ignore the one thing I felt bad about—disrespecting my mother on the phone. When I called to apologize, she was rather cold to me. I assumed she thought I was in the wrong but I talked with her anyway. I was sure it was hurting my parents that Kamille and I were at odds; they had always been adamant that we be a close-knit family. And we had been up until now. Our being adopted had never been an issue until a few years ago, when Kamille began demanding to know who her biological parents were. My parents had been unable to offer more than the name of the agency from which she'd been adopted.

But Kamille and I weren't my parents' only worry. My seventeen-year-old brother, Julian, was considering skipping college to play professional baseball. According to my mother, sports agents were seeking him out, as were college recruiters. I knew she was anxious to talk to Malik about Julian's future, so I kindly gave her his cell phone number.

As much as I didn't want to, I was forced to communicate with Kamille and Malik on some level because we had to discuss the opening of the club. By the end of the day I figured the best way to handle it would be to send them e-mails. Before I left work, I typed up an e-mail to Malik and Kamille to update them on the progress of the club. I waited for a response, but there was none.

By Wednesday I was so busy at work that I was actually relieved when I received a call from G-dog asking me to go out. I assumed we'd go to a late dinner and maybe the movies, but was surprised when we pulled up in front of the chaos of Front and Market Streets, where new clubs were always springing up overnight. He was no Malik when it came to a night on the town, but there was no need for me to complain because I'd never even bothered to ask where we were going in the first place. G-dog didn't bother to find a parking lot, he just handed a valet the keys to his black Dodge Ram 1500, with a Hemi, as he'd told me when I asked about the gunning noise the truck made. Stepping out of the truck, I began to feel like all eyes were on me, asking the question of what I was doing with G-dog.

It was NBA Wednesday inside Club Suede, but there didn't seem to be a basketball player in sight. Another problem with nightclubs, I noted, was that the so-called special invited guests—celebrities—never bothered to show up. This could give a club a bad reputation, but it would not happen at Teaz. The sounds of the remix of Fifty Cent's "In Da Club" blared throughout the club, but the music was ignored by most of the crowd, who were doing more socializing than dancing. We eventually found a space to sit on one of the soft leathery couches. While G-dog ordered drinks I took in the club's furnishings—the granite bar that stood in the middle of the floor and the waterfall that ran against the back wall. It was a trendy place, but none of these clubs would be able to compare to Teaz when it opened.

After two glasses of Merlot I began to relax and enjoy the evening talking with G-dog and his friends. I didn't even mind when I felt G-dog grinding up against me while he echoed Juvenile in my ear, telling me that he liked the way I worked that thing. . . . That's when I realized what I'd been missing about this business. It hadn't been fun for me for a long time. Probably since I'd met Malik and had decided to go into the business end of it. So rather than continue to analyze every aspect of the night, I became Tiffany the patron and went with the flow of the crowd.

Around eleven, as we were leaving, I stopped in my tracks when I was practically knocked over by my sister. I wasn't sure how to react. But before I had to make a decision, G-dog saved me.

"C'mon, just speak to her and keep moving. You don't need all these niggas to know your business," he suggested from behind me.

"Hello, Kamille," I said, noticing she was with a guy I'd never seen before. Not only was she drunk, but I could tell from the redness of her eyes she'd been smoking weed.

"Yeah, what's up," she said loudly as she passed by. I was afraid that if I lingered too long we might get into a fight, so I allowed G-dog to keep pushing me toward the door.

Once we were back in G-dog's truck and I'd taken a few deep breaths, he asked me if I'd mind making another stop. I was still a bit shaken from my run-in with Kamille so it didn't matter to me. Following behind one of his friends, we rode around the corner to Buffalo Billiards, an upscale pool hall on Chestnut Street. When we pulled up out front it seemed as if people had been anticipating G-dog's arrival.

"Looks like you could use a drink. What you say?" he asked, once he sat me at a table.

"Good idea. A Merlot would be cool."

"I got something for you. Mack, make this girl a panty ripper," he yelled across the room to the bartender.

"A what?"

Bending over and placing his hands on my shoulders, he said, "It's a lotta rum and a little bit of pineapple juice."

"Well, I hope it's not going to make me want to rip my panties off."

"Don't worry, if you start feeling like that, I'll do it for you."

I hadn't been to a pool hall in years and had never even heard of this place. It was filled with men, drinking and taking their shots, accompanied by beautiful women who stood close by. The pool hall took up two levels, each complete with about five tables. Even though I told G-dog that I hadn't shot pool in over six years, he insisted that I pick up a stick. We played pool until I downed my fourth panty ripper, then we moved on to Snyder Avenue to sober up on coffee and pancakes at Melrose Diner.

During the course of the week I spoke with G-dog often, and he convinced me that he actually did have something to offer Teaz. He was part-owner of a new security company that he felt was quite capable of providing security personnel for the club. I thought it was a good idea since we'd yet to select an agency, which meant less work for me, though finding security for the club had been one of Kamille's responsibilities. I agreed to look over G-dog's proposal and told him I'd pass it along for my attorney's review.

Since I had to meet soon with my Teaz partners to go over club business, I figured I'd bring this up at the meeting as well. But setting up the meeting was where I was having a problem. I didn't think I could handle seeing Malik and

Kamille in the same room. Then I remembered that Malik traveled the last Thursday of every month to South Carolina to visit his alma mater, Clemson University, where he was chairman of the Alumni Committee. I figured that would be the perfect time to hold a meeting in one of Platinum Image's conference rooms. That way I could just send any final papers over to his office for his review and signature. As for Kamille, G-dog said not to worry because he'd be there with me.

On the evening of the meeting I set out champagne glasses and two bottles of Moët before everyone arrived. Growing anxious at the thought of having to face my sister in such close quarters, I poured myself a glass of champagne and was on my second drink when Kamille and Essence arrived, at exactly 7:00 P.M. I was sure Essence was responsible for their promptness because Kamille could never get anywhere on time.

"What's up, Tiffany?" Kamille asked, her voice shaky.

"Hey," I answered, purposely keeping my back to her.

Essence walked over and hugged me, leaving my sister unsure of what to do since I was ignoring her.

"Tiffany, can I say something to you?" Kamille asked from behind me.

I whipped around and let my glare tell her what kind of mood I was in.

"What could you possibly say after sleeping with Malik? Huh, what can you say, Kamille? What the fuck could you possibly say?"

"You've got everything wrong. If you'd listen to me, I could tell you what happened."

"I don't have to listen to shit. I know exactly what happened—you screwed my boyfriend, had his baby, and forgot to tell me."

"Tiffany, why are you doing this? Kamille is your sister," Essence said.

"My sister?" I placed my hands on the table for support and stared into Kamille's sad and colorless face. "That bitch isn't my sister." I knew I'd cut her deep with that remark. Since we were kids, Kamille and our brother and I had vowed to stick together as a family.

Luckily, G-dog, his lawyer, and Jeff, our director of operations, broke up the encounter before I tossed a paperweight at her. When G-dog walked over to me, I surprised him and everyone else by planting a long and juicy kiss on his lips. When I pulled away I asked, "Are we still on for tonight?"

He kissed me again and said, "As soon as we can get outta here."

I didn't even bother to gauge their reaction.

When everyone was seated I passed out briefs that updated them on the progress of the club, which was due to open at the end of the summer. Kamille and Essence were both surprised that G-dog had been included in this meeting and that he had a contract on the table to provide security for the club. It wasn't as if it was a bad idea, just that he was offering it. They knew that final decisions were mine since I was the one who'd invested the most money. The next stage of the game was where things went wrong.

We were midway through discussions when I heard the door downstairs open. I shot a glance at G-dog that told him to go see who it was, but before he could get up Malik walked in. A gloom descended on the room.

Cutting my eyes to my sister to see her reaction, I saw her pop something in her mouth, then take a big gulp of champagne. She seemed just as nervous as I was. I assumed she was having one of the headaches she often complained about. Essence, on the other hand, was smirking at me, as if daring me to continue with my game. G-dog slouched down in his chair and became a shrinking violet inside of his Yankees baseball cap.

Malik strolled into the conference room wearing a gray suit and a white shirt, open at the collar. He sat his briefcase on the floor beside the door. My eyes rested on his face as he used his hand to smooth the hair from his mustache down to his goatee. I tried to ignore Malik and tell myself that I hated him. But I knew that was a lie.

"I'm sorry I'm late, everyone, but I just flew back into town."

He circled the table and leaned over and kissed me on the cheek, forcing me to smell his Burberry-Britt cologne. Part of me wanted to lash out and tell him that I was not his to kiss and the other part wanted to pull him toward me and hold on. Instead, I stood up and brought a bottle of champagne to the table and began refilling everyone's glasses.

"Malik, we're finished, but feel free to take your copy of the paperwork with you," I said.

Everyone was quiet, watching as I displayed this false act of bravery. But Malik wasn't budging. I returned to my seat, not sure what to do with myself. As I sat across the table from

Malik and my sister, visions of them in bed together floated through my mind. I poured myself another drink when what I really wanted to do was run out of the room.

"Thanks, but I'll read them here," he said, as G-dog's attorney slid the sheaf of papers across the table.

Pulling his reading glasses from his inside coat pocket, Malik began reviewing the papers. I knew he wouldn't sign them, though not because anything was wrong; he was posturing to let everyone know that he had legal control over Teaz Entertainment.

I watched my sister pour herself another glass of champagne, and that's when I realized that we were the only ones drinking. When Essence broke the unbearable silence by announcing that she was leaving, my sister quickly rose from her seat and stood beside her. G-dog nodded to his lawyer and they also began to exit the room. It was obvious that Malik wasn't planning to leave until he talked to me.

Essence passed by me on her way out the door and whispered in my ear, "You better slow down on all that drinking."

I could feel Malik's eyes follow me as I walked G-dog to the top of the stairs.

"I'll see you later?" he asked.

"For sure."

"You gonna be alright with him?"

I pushed back his cap and said, "Yeah, go on. I'm fine. I'll call you when I get through here."

I walked back into the room, turning my attention to Malik. I skirted by him and sauntered over to the credenza to pour another flute of champagne.

"The meeting is over, Malik," I said with my back to him.

"Do you really think I'm going to let G-dog or whatever the hell his name is have anything to do with Teaz?"

"You don't have a choice. It's really my decision." I could hear him roll his chair back and get up.

He came up behind me and placed his hands on my shoulders, probably trying to hold down the beast that had grown in me.

Leaning into my ear, he said, "I'm not letting you walk out of here until you listen to what I have to say."

"I'm listening," I said, turning my head away, trying to shake the sound of his voice out of my ear.

His warm hands touched my face to wipe the one tear that rolled from the corner of my eye. "Baby, I'm not asking you to forgive me. I just want you to hear me out."

Still I wouldn't turn around.

"Tiffany, you are the only woman I love, that I've ever loved. I don't want to lose you. If I could take back that weekend I had with your sister, I would. But I won't let it tear down everything we've built together."

"What if Kareem's your son?"

"Then I'll handle it however you want me to. Whatever is best for us."

"And what about my sister?"

He moved from behind me and leaned against the credenza, facing me, his hand resting on my hips.

"Malik, this isn't about what's best for me. It's about your son." The word got caught in my throat. I sipped the warm Moët.

"We don't know that yet. Can't you at least wait until we know for sure?" he asked, his voice strained, trying to soothe the hurt I'm sure he knew I was feeling.

Tears rolled down my face. I wanted to tell him I loved him, that I would wait it out, but this wasn't just another woman's baby, this was my sister's. My hands began to tremble and I stood there shaking. I felt myself slipping into that space where all those thoughts of him and Kamille lived.

He reached out, pulling me into his arms. "Oh, my God. I miss you, Tiffany. I miss being beside you every night, making love to you."

Somehow I'd nestled myself into that nook in his arms that belonged only to me, but my mind played another trick and told me that maybe my sister had found a place in his arms, too. I fought to get out of his embrace unsuccessfully; he calmed my fight by cradling my head and running his tongue across my lips.

"I love you, woman. Let me take you home."

And with that I hungrily kissed him, devouring his words. "I miss you so much, Malik. Do you know how bad this all hurts?"

"I know, baby, and I'm sorry. Damn, am I sorry."

He massaged my shoulders with his warm hands, then held up my hair and kissed the back of my neck. My heart was pounding against my chest, wanting him to hurry up and make love to me before I remembered why we were there. Pulling my blouse apart, he lifted one breast out of my bra and sucked hard while kneading the other. I wanted to shake loose of him but he held on to me, tight, until he felt my resistance melt away. He then eased his hands under my skirt and slid them down inside my pantyhose, pushing them over my thighs and down to my ankles. Then he knelt and kissed me on the fine hairs that covered my womanhood. I couldn't wait any longer.

"Maaa . . . I . . . I . . ."

He rose and I unbuckled his pants, reaching inside for what I needed. I stroked up and down his hard shaft until he responded by biting down on my nipple. I guided him between my open legs.

"I know, baby, I know."

With my eyes closed I wrapped my legs around his back, taking him in farther. Digging my fingers into his shoulders, I cried out, "I love you. I love you, Malik."

Holding on to the cheeks of Malik's firm ass, I felt tears stream down my face as he screamed out my name, causing my orgasm to rock against his.

When we were done, I lay against him panting, until slowly Malik eased himself out of me. Breathless and empty, I fell back against the wall. Feeling the weight of his body and his rapidly thumping heartbeat, I squeezed my eyes tight, trying to figure out how I'd let this happen.

"Can we please let this all go so I can come home?" Malik asked, while cleaning himself off with a tissue.

Then it registered why Malik and I were there, making love in the conference room, and from a distant corner of my mind, the madness and hurt all came back.

"Tiff, baby, you hear me?"

I started pulling down my skirt and adjusting the buttons

on my blouse. "Come home?" My suppressed anger had returned. "You don't have a home with me."

"Tiffany, what are you saying? You just—"

"I just what?" I asked, looking under the table for my purse.

He looked at me, confused and hurt that his lovemaking hadn't been able to solve our problems.

"Tiffany, you wanted me as much as I wanted you tonight. You know you don't want this to be over."

"You're wrong, Malik. This right here, what happened was a mistake."

He fastened his belt and slid his arms into his suit jacket.

"That's it, Tiffany. I'm not begging anymore," he said, walking toward the door.

"I hate you, Malik! I hate you!" I yelled after him.

3

SPRING FLING

I never met up with G-dog that night. I just went home and drank until I passed out. When I finally spoke with him a couple weeks later, rather than ask me why I'd been a no-show, he was calling to invite me to his parents' place in the Hamptons.

Arriving at their beachfront property on Friday night was like coming out of the cocoon of pain and confusion that had become my life. I was hoping that maybe on Long Island, away from Philly, I'd have some time to sort everything out.

G-dog's parents' house was in Montauk, just a few blocks from the marina. The Haneys' pockets had to be very deep for them to afford this four-bedroom house, complete with a swimming pool and a hot tub, and surrounded by flowering trees and brightly colored flowerbeds. Nanny, their Filipino housekeeper, greeted us. G-dog told me she had been with their family since he was a toddler.

I would've been satisfied to spend the weekend sitting on the porch swing and sipping Long Island iced teas, but G-dog had other plans. He had some friends who were stopping by, so I offered to fix dinner, but he said that people like us, whatever that meant, didn't cook in the Hamptons. We either ate out or ordered in.

By 8:00 P.M. four of his friends arrived, couples I assumed, though I couldn't be sure since they all seemed so intimate with each other. I hoped that didn't mean G-dog was into anything kinky. Up until now he hadn't forced the issue of our having sex. I'd tried taking Essence's advice by keeping my drinking to a minimum, but G-dog insisted that I taste a concoction he called Incredible Hulk, which was Moët with a shot of Hennessy on top. It would've been a little too strong for me under normal circumstances; however my being in the Hamptons with G-dog was far from being normal. Plus, I easily helped it along by taking a few tokes of a blunt.

As the night progressed and once everyone was sufficiently stoned, we headed out to a local spot called the Greentree Tavern. The place was filled with mostly young white kids and future entrepreneurs. G-dog introduced me to everyone like I was his trophy. It was easy to see that in this town, among this crowd, he thrived being their hero from the big city. After everyone recovered from the surprise of seeing G-dog with me, which he said was because he usually brought white girls to those places, the spot returned to normal. By that point I was feeling nice and giddy and could not have cared less what people thought about me.

D12 and Eminem played crisply from an iPod connected to speakers that sat in the corners of the bar. And somehow the lyrics of being ". . . the lead singer of my band" and "I'll be the man" mimicked G-dog's behavior and personality. There wasn't much room to move around and twice I was offered Ecstasy and cocaine, which I declined because I wasn't that drunk or that desperate to drown out my thoughts. For the most part I sat drinking watered-down gin and tonics. As I watched G-dog I realized that his persona often fluctuated between some fake-ass bad boy and the proper politician that I'm sure his father was hoping he'd become.

It was after two in the morning when we parked in front of the house. My high had begun to wear off and was slowly being replaced by a headache. Beside me G-dog, who reeked of alcohol and cigarette smoke, was pawing all over me. We'd only made it to the front porch and he had me plastered against the wall of the house. I guessed this meant we were having sex.

"Girl, I'm going to tear this ass up," he growled into my ear.

I almost had to laugh at him when I realized how high he was. He never got this high back home. I hoped he hadn't been snorting coke or, worse, taken one of those Ecstasy pills.

"Can we at least get inside the house? How's that?" I asked, then sat down on the porch swing. G-dog unsuccessfully fished in his pocket for his house keys.

"Fuck going in the house."

He stumbled over to me and pushed my legs open by

putting his knees between mine. He bent forward, his hands roughly playing with my breasts. I began to really convince myself that there was no reason for me to be faithful to Malik or that sham of an engagement we'd had. Plus, I was curious to see if I could enjoy sex with another man.

"G-dog, I wanna go inside," I said, feeling myself get aroused. I gazed up at a sky that was so lit by stars that it could've been daytime, as G-dog's head made its way between my breasts.

"I can't wait that long. I gotta have this shit now."

"Well, slow down and let me do this, okay?" I said.

I pulled him up on his feet and slid his shorts down to his ankles. Slowly, I lowered my mouth onto his swollen and red dick. I could've sworn when I looked up that his eyes rolled to the back of his head.

Moaning, he held on to my hair, using it to guide my head up and down. G-dog wasn't exceptionally large, which enabled me to easily take his entire dick in my mouth, covering it with my lips. It didn't take long, maybe five minutes before I could tell from his labored breathing that he was about to come.

"Wait, wait," he murmured, then reached in his pocket and pulled out a condom.

He pulled me up off my knees and before I knew it his strong arms were bending me over the railing. I was expecting nothing more than a drunken fuck and I was absolutely right because he pushed my panties to the side and rammed himself inside me. I held on to the banister as he pushed me farther over the railing until I thought I was going to puke from being turned upside down. As I made an effort to stand up I heard him take a deep breath, then he thrust himself hard inside me and it was over. So much for thinking his lovemaking could replace Malik's.

When G-dog woke up in the morning I was in the kitchen making scrambled eggs and brewing coffee. I had no idea what he ate for breakfast because this was our first morning together.

"I hope I'm the one who gave you a big appetite," he bragged, walking into the kitchen in his boxers.

"Not really," I joked, wanting to ask him how that could be possible when he'd come so fast last night.

"What? We'll see about that."

"I mean, you were quite drunk."

"Watch and see how I'm gonna take care of your little sweet ass the rest of the weekend, Ms. Tiffany Johnson. You can be sure of that."

"That's what I'm hoping." I would have said more, but I was surprised by the housekeeper coming down the stairs. I certainly did not want her to hear our conversation.

After G-dog teased with her about having found himself a wife, which I didn't think was so funny, I changed the subject.

"What you need, baby girl?"

"I need to ask you a favor, but I can understand if you say no," I said, setting the plate of eggs and toast in front of him.

"What is it? You know I'd do anything you want."

"It's my family. They're having a cookout on Monday and

I have to go because in addition to it being Memorial Day, it's also a party for my brother. Will you go with me?"

"Damn, that's right. Young Huli's gone to play in the minors!"

Young Huli was the nickname my brother had picked up in the streets and on the baseball field. But how did G-dog know he was going into the league already? I guessed it was because the news had been in the sports section of every Philadelphia newspaper and Young Huli had already purchased a Mercedes SL55.

"Can I take that as a yes?" I asked, moving over to sit on his lap.

"Sure, I'll go. But will your sister be there, and . . . ?"

"Yeah, and maybe Malik, too."

"Don't worry. I'll be there, but you going to have to pay."

"How so?" I asked, as I squirmed in his lap, hoping that he'd be a better lover than the night before.

"You already know."

We spent the rest of the afternoon in bed with him doing a good job of satisfying me, or so I led him to believe. Frustrated, I told myself that with practice maybe he'd become a better lover. Once I heard him snoring, I showered and headed out of the house, curious to see what the Hamptons were all about. I found a ten-speed bike in the garage and rode toward the marina. The streets of Montauk were crowded with every type of luxury car imaginable, and there were lots of shops and sidewalk cafés. Even with all its pretentiousness, there was something about the Hamptons that I liked, that pulled me in.

At the beach, I paused to soak in the beautifully clear day with the sun glistening off the ocean. I sat in the sand for more than an hour thinking about how my life had changed. I wondered what Malik was doing at that very moment and if he would like the Hamptons. Then my thinking began to change as my sister's face entered the picture. Perhaps I should've heard them out, at least my sister. I mean, what would I have done in their situation? It was all way too much for me to figure out.

But there was no denying that I missed my life with Malik, all the little things that made up our relationship. There'd be no tee times on Saturday mornings or football games for me to complain about, no NBA finals parties. I couldn't imagine attending church services on Sundays without him. Every morning Malik would try coaxing me to work out with him and every morning I'd decline, roll over, and go back to sleep. Yet when he returned he'd make breakfast for the two of us before heading off to work.

Just as I was about to convince myself that I should talk to Malik, I noticed five white limos pulling up to the Atlantica, which had to be the most beautiful place for someone to hold a wedding reception. A wedding party got out of the limos, and I watched the happy couple kissing and posing for pictures, their laughter spilling over into my thoughts. I imagined I would've been as happy or even happier had Malik and I made it to our wedding day. I'd planned to have a small wedding party and a ceremony at my mother's church. It was the honeymoon that Malik and I had been saving for, ten days of passionate lovemaking on a secluded island. A heaviness settled in my chest. Why had everything

in my life gone wrong? It was hard to have hope that somewhere in the future happiness was still a possibility for me.

On the way back to the house I took a wrong turn and
discovered a small cottage with a FOR RENT sign posted in the
yard. Even though I had no interest in leaving Philadelphia,
the house still piqued my interest. I dismounted and walked
through the gate. Stepping onto the porch, I peered in the
long rectangular windows, which were half-covered with
paper. Inside I could see yellow paint peeling from the walls.
I walked toward the back of the house, maneuvering around
overgrown bushes that scratched my legs. Once in the back I
was able to see into a dingy black and white tiled kitchen.
The living room was partially in view and had a sagging ceiling and a cracked red brick fireplace. I couldn't tell the number of bedrooms. Some old furniture was strewn about as
well as a bunch of trash. It certainly looked like a house that
somebody forgot about. I wrote down the realtor's number
and headed back to G-dog.

We'd only spent two days in the Hamptons, but G-dog
had thoroughly gotten on my nerves. He was constantly
telling me what I should do with the club and how I should
invest my money. He was almost insistent that I replace
Malik as my attorney for Teaz. I didn't need to ask if he had
somebody in mind for the job. There was no way I was
allowing a stranger that far into my personal life and finan-
cial affairs. Malik was the only one who knew the details of
all that. By Monday, even though I wasn't quite ready to
attend my parents' cookout, I was definitely ready to get out
of such close quarters with G-dog.

Speeding down the New Jersey Turnpike, we took Exit 4 to my parents' home in Cherry Hill. To ease my frazzled nerves I lit up a half-smoked blunt he had sitting in the ashtray, pulling the smoke so deep into my lungs that I started coughing.

"You better slow down on that shit."

I ignored him. Who was he to tell me how to handle my life?

"Is that nigga gonna be there or what?"

"Why do you always have to use that word?"

"What? Nigga? After what he did to you, I didn't think you cared what I called him."

"What I meant is—I mean—I don't care what you call him. Anyway, I don't know for sure. I don't consider him part of my family."

But even as I said those words they turned bitter in my mouth. I realized that Malik could very well be part of my family if he actually was Kareem's father. It wasn't the time to get caught up in those thoughts, especially as we pulled up to my parents' already crowded cul-de-sac. I took a deep breath and climbed out of G-dog's truck.

My parents' yard was decorated in red, white, and blue holiday regalia and a huge flag waved from the porch roof. The neighbors' kids were jumping double Dutch out front, while the teenage boys were playing basketball at a portable hoop in the middle of the street.

The smell of barbeque ribs began wafting from the backyard. It put a smile on my face. If nothing else I knew I'd get a home-cooked meal. My mouth began to water at the

thought of my mother's potato salad and homemade strawberry shortcake. Maybe seeing my sister wouldn't be so bad
after all.

Entering the backyard, I didn't see my parents nor my sister right away so I figured they were probably in the house. I
was glad to have a few more minutes before I had to face
them.

I waded through the crowd, giving hugs and kisses to my
aunts, uncles, and my parents' neighbors, until I got to my
brother. Julian, looking like a young Derek Jeter, was
stretched out in a lounge chair next to the aboveground pool.
Some woman who looked to be my age was rubbing him
down with suntan lotion.

"What's going on, big sis?"

"Nothing much. What about you, Young Huli?" I teased,
while looking around at the kids who splashed about in the
pool.

"You know your little brother 'bout to do his thing in a
big way."

"Yeah, well, just don't get too damn big."

It was hard for us to carry on a conversation because the
neighborhood kids were flocking to Young Huli and making
pests of themselves by asking him to come over to the field
and play ball with them.

"Why'd you bring dude with you?" my brother asked,
nodding toward G-dog, who was already in conversation
with someone who recognized him as the DA's son.

"Damn, he's just a friend. You act like Malik is the only
man this family recognizes."

"Guess so."

I flipped him the finger behind my back as I walked away. That's when I saw my parents standing over the grill. I grabbed a Bud Light from the cooler and slid up next to them. My father was in his white apron and chef hat, dousing the chicken with sauce as my mother stood beside him, probably telling him how she wanted it cooked.

"Hey, Mom, Dad," I said, easing myself between them.

My mother kissed me on the cheek and appeared to be happy to see me, but my father didn't hide his disappointment at seeing me with an unfamiliar man.

"Why the hell have you brought another man to our family function?"

"Dad, G-dog is the district attorney's son."

He turned to face me. "I don't care who he is, he's not part of this family."

"You act as if you don't know about Malik and Kamille."

My mother conveniently slipped away, something she always did when my father disciplined us.

"I'm aware of the circumstances, but you're not making any sense with the way you've been carrying on. I hear you have been drinking and God only knows what else. I want you to stop this foolishness right now and talk with your sister. And for God's sake, please talk to Malik. The poor boy is miserable."

I looked around the yard, suddenly feeling like I didn't belong. Who did my parents think they were fooling with this family of misfits? Kamille wasn't really my sister, and all these aunts, uncles, and cousins weren't any blood kin to me.

Maybe my sister had been right to look for her birth parents. Maybe I needed to find out who my real family was, too.

"Why is this all of a sudden my fault?"

"Tiffany, I thought you were smart. You used to have control over your life. Your behavior lately has been ridiculous."

"Dad, you really don't understand, do you?" I retorted through the heat and smoke that rose from the grill, making my eyes water.

My nephews' voices broke through what was about to become a heated argument.

"Auntie Tiff, Auntie Tiff, where you been?" Raphael and Anthony asked, barreling out the back door, grabbing hold of my legs.

My natural reaction was to kneel down and pull them into my arms. Choking back tears, I told them I'd been busy and that I'd come see them soon. I looked over and saw my mother grilling G-dog, and it seemed almost as if she were guiding him out of the backyard. I marched over to them.

"Mom, what are you doing?"

"Nothing. I was just telling your friend that you're getting married next year."

"How could you think I'd still marry Malik? And why are you discussing my business with *him?*" I screamed, pointing my finger from my mother to G-dog. Now I was treating G-dog like an outsider, too. This was all turning out very bad.

"Well, somebody has to talk some sense into you," my mother screamed back at me.

I was about to lash out at my mother when I felt a little hand folding into mine.

"Auntie Tiff, where's Uncle Malik?" Kareem asked. Kamille came up behind him, looking surprised and embarrassed, as if she hadn't expected me to show up. I stepped away from her.

"Uh, hey, Tiffany," she said, without looking me in the eye.

She didn't seem her usual self. She looked tired and almost as if she'd lost some weight. I guessed she was suffering with this, too, but she'd brought it all on herself.

"Come on, Kareem. Auntie Tiff doesn't want to talk right now," she said, taking him by the arm and leading him over to the pool.

I could see everyone beginning to stare at me as if I was a crazed woman. Maybe I was. I shouted out across the yard, loud enough for everyone to hear: "What the hell is wrong with everybody? Doesn't anybody realize that I'm the one who got hurt?"

"Tiffany, you lower your voice. We have company here. I won't allow you to go on a tirade in front of the entire family," my father spat at me.

"Who you fooling, Dad? Ain't nobody out here family. You should've never adopted me in the first place."

The backyard quieted.

That's when I felt Young Huli's hand on my back, pushing me out of the yard toward the front of the house. "Tiffany, come on. Let's go."

"Everybody wants to be on their side. Nobody cares how I feel."

My father walked up close to me and, between clenched

teeth, said, "Get out of here right now, young lady, and don't come back until you can talk some sense."

I was livid. How dare my family turn on me? That was it—if they didn't want me around, then they'd never see me again.

By now my brother had sat me down on the glider on my parents' front porch, causing my cousins who were sitting on it to quickly scatter.

"What the hell is up with you, sis? Why you acting like this? Kamille's boys are back there crying and shit because they didn't get a chance to speak with you."

"Julian, you don't understand. You got it all wrong."

Frustrated, he sat down next to me, put his feet up on the table, and draped his arm around my shoulders. "That's bullshit. I know what's up. You can't deal with this shit on your own. You need your family."

"I don't need anybody," I said, while watching G-dog standing beside his truck talking on the cell phone. He and his cell were never far apart.

"Yeah, well, sis, I hate to be the one to tell you, but all birds have to return to the flock sooner or later. I mean, what about Kamille? Man, she's hurting, too."

"Julian, I do want to understand, but I can't get past what she did to me," I cried.

"She ain't done nothing intentional. Man, that shit happened years ago. Kareem probably ain't even his. Plus, you can't let that come between you and Kamille. We family."

Listening to my brother, I realized that maybe my father was right. What was I doing? I didn't want to lose my family. They really were all I had. I just couldn't figure out how to get a grip on everything. I didn't even feel like I knew who I was anymore. I was not the Tiffany Johnson of just a few weeks ago, when everything in my life had been perfect. I'd been the epitome of a young businesswoman on the rise. All that had come crumbling down because of Malik and Kamille's indiscretion.

I could no longer control my tears and was sobbing loudly. I didn't see G-dog when he stepped onto the porch.

"What the hell you say to her?" G-dog demanded of my brother.

"Whoa, buddy. I don't think you know who the fuck you talking to."

I'd never heard my brother talk like that, never seen him stand up to another man. G-dog immediately backed down as my brother stood up, towering over him.

"Listen, man. All I'm saying is you got her upset," G-dog said.

"Fuck you, pretty boy. She going through some shit that she don't wanna deal with, and if you can't help her, then step the fuck off."

I jumped in between them. "Julian, I'm okay. Please, I can't take another argument."

"You want me to take you home, sis?"

"No, I'm fine. Now, go ahead, Young Huli. Go have some fun," I teased, trying to make light of everything.

He kissed me on the cheek, glared at G-dog, and walked down the steps.

I turned to G-dog. "Can you please get me out of here?"

4

SHIFTING GEARS

With everything that had taken place recently, the last thing I wanted to do was leave Platinum Images. Unfortunately, it was too late. Tuesday would be my last day. When I came in that morning I found my office draped in balloons, flowers, and a stack of gifts. My coworkers were all in great moods. Maybe they were happy I was leaving, which was understandable, as I hadn't been the best person to work with lately. But these were the people, especially Michael and Kendra, who over the past six years had been more than coworkers. They'd been my friends and certainly didn't deserve my erratic behavior. So I put on a smiling face and acted as if I knew what I was doing by leaving the only place that provided me with stability.

The morning was filled with phone calls from vendors and clients, all wishing me success with Teaz. All was going well until I received a call from the contractor working on Teaz. He told me that they would have to stop work if I didn't have at least the occupancy and zoning permits. The first person I thought to call was Malik, but not wanting him to think I needed him and unsure of how the conversation would go, I sent him an e-mail instead. His response was, "I'll see what I can do."

Sensing that meant he'd do nothing, I called G-dog next. He'd gone out of town for a few days, so I left him a message, knowing that he'd do whatever he could to make sure the club opened on time.

By 1:00 P.M. I was ready to go out with Michael and Kendra for my farewell lunch. They'd always been good to me and had been holding up my end of the office for the last weeks while I suffered through my personal life. We took the short walk down to Sonoma's with Kendra chattering away about her vacation plans. Once we were seated all eyes turned to me, and I knew they were waiting for the reason for my sadness.

"So this is it, huh? You're glad to be getting away from us?" Michael asked.

"Come on, don't push me out the door that fast."

"I'm not, but it's obvious you really haven't been here the last few weeks."

Kendra chimed in. "Yeah, so what's up, Tiffany? I mean, I don't work for you anymore, so we can talk girl talk."

"It's just me and Malik. We're having some problems, major problems. But I don't wanna talk about it."

"You're still getting married, aren't you?" she asked, while the waitress stood waiting to take our order.

"I'm not sure."

When they noticed the tears welling up in my eyes, they changed the subject.

"Anyway, what's up with the two of you?" I asked. "I hear you've got a new boyfriend hanging around the office, Kendra."

"One of Michael's friends," she answered, knowing she had caught me off guard with her answer.

"Michael's friends?" I said it with shock because all these years I'd assumed Michael wasn't into women, thus didn't have friends who were interested either.

"Tell her, Michael."

"Well, Tiffany, I hate to disappoint you, but I do have some male friends who aren't gay."

We all broke into laughter, and I realized how much I was going to miss these two and the camaraderie they provided.

By 6:00 P.M. I'd turned off my computer for the last time, had packed up my office with all its trinkets and memories, and was sliding down in my chair, scared to leave the building. Hiding my face in my hands, I wondered how I could gather up enough strength to see me through the next few months till Teaz opened in September. And what would happen once it did open? Maybe opening a nightclub was too risky. Maybe there was too much competition across the city for Teaz to be successful. What if I lost all of my, and everyone else's, investment? Before I could allow myself to get absorbed in my misgivings, Kendra buzzed me over the intercom. I had a call from our CEO, Sasha Borianni.

Sasha had been on an extended leave of absence from the firm to get married and travel across the country with her husband. She'd been a great mentor for me and I'd learned a lot from her, not just about the business of public relations but also about life itself. I'd probably emulated her in her business and personal relationships more that I should have because she was just so amazing to me in all that she had accomplished.

"Sasha, hey, where are you?" I asked, excited to talk to her.

"I'm not even sure I know. Trent has planned this entire vacation. But I don't want to talk about me. It's you I'm concerned about. I hear you've been drifting around the office like you're not happy to be taking on the world."

"I think I've taken on too much this time. I'm just not ready for this. I mean, who am I to think—"

"What the hell are you talking about? I hope this second-guessing your decision doesn't have anything to do with a man. Are you and Malik okay?"

"Sasha, we're far from okay. It's over with us, but I don't want to bore you with the details on that and—"

"Listen to me."

I fell silent.

"Tiffany, we go through life trying to balance our personal life with our business life, not really understanding how one complements the other. You have to use one to build the other. Remember, you have to play to win."

"I'm not sure what you mean," I said, trying to find some hope in her words.

"When you came to the firm you were full of ideas, and the only thing you had to go on was your self-confidence.

What I'm saying, Tiffany, is if your personal life is a mess, then take all that negative energy and put it into your club and I swear to you that you'll come out on top. It's worked for me."

I knew Sasha was right, but it would take some time for me to figure out how to put her advice to use. "Thank you, Sasha. Now, get back to your honeymoon. We'll get together when you return."

I drove home that evening with my truck filled with my stuff from the office, and when I pulled into the parking lot at home I was surprised to see Malik's car parked in my space.

When I stepped through the front door Malik was sitting in his tattered brown recliner, patting Bruiser, who stood in front of him wagging his tail. It seemed the only time that dog was happy was when his master was around.

"Hey, Malik," I said, trying not to notice how good he looked dressed in a pair of black linen pants and a white button-down linen shirt. His skin was tanned, his hair freshly cut, and his mustache and goatee neatly trimmed. I wanted to wrap my arms around him.

"I tried to call you but nobody answered, so I figured it was a good time for me to come by and get my things."

"It's not a problem. You want something to drink?"

"A cold beer if you have one."

He followed me into the kitchen. My stopping short caused his body to accidentally bump into mine.

"I'm sorry," he said, backing away as if the last thing he wanted to do was touch me. He walked around me and down the stairs into the basement, where we kept the beer.

While he was downstairs I thought of all the things I

wanted to say to him. I wanted to ask if he'd had the tests done but was too afraid to hear his answer. I wanted to ask if he was dating anyone, even though I'd already heard he'd been seen out to dinner with a woman. The last thing I wanted to do was start an argument.

I watched as he went back and forth to the car moving his stuff out of the house, Bruiser trotting behind him. The only thing of his he left behind was the recliner in the living room. After he carried out the last of his things, he took a drink of his Corona.

"Malik, can we talk for a minute?" I asked, sitting on the edge of the sofa.

Pausing in the kitchen doorway, he asked, "What is it, Tiffany? You couldn't want to talk now. I mean, you've made it clear you don't give a damn about me with the way you've moved on with your life."

Why was he doing this? Couldn't he see I was ready to talk? But no, he wanted to make this difficult, wanted to make me pay for not listening to him in the first place.

"I just wanted to know how you've been."

"I've been quite fine. I hear you have a new boyfriend."

He caught me off guard with his response, and I wasn't sure why I'd even entertained the possibility that we could have a civil conversation.

"G-dog and I are friends."

"Not according to his daddy."

"What are you talking about? His father doesn't know anything about me," I said, not understanding why the DA would mention me to Malik.

"Remember, Tiffany, I attend some of the same functions and sit on the same boards as the honorable Mr. Greg Haney II. I must say he seems pretty damn proud that you're part of 'his family,' to put it in his words."

I had to admit to myself that I was flattered to hear that Mr. Haney felt this way. I wondered what G-dog had told him about me and began looking forward to meeting the handsome man I'd seen on TV.

Malik moved out of my way as I walked past him into the kitchen. I removed two Coronas from the carton, handing him one and opening the other for myself. By now he was standing close to the front door, ready to leave.

I made sure to take the edge out of my voice before responding.

"I'm not sure what G-dog's father is talking about, but I did want to ask you something."

"Go ahead. Say what's on your mind, Tiffany."

I cleared my throat as I sat down on the couch. "Have you gotten the test results back yet?"

He gulped down half his beer. "I figured that's what this was all about. You know what? Why don't you ask your sister?"

"What? You bastard! That is your son, isn't it? How could you do this to me?"

"Why is this situation always about you? You're not the only one who's been hurt. What about your sister, Tiffany? Hell, what about me? You think somebody planned this shit?"

I jumped up from the sofa and stepped in front of him,

my face close to his. "Malik, I don't give a fuck about you or my sister. After what you did to me, I don't ever want to hear a damn thing you have to say."

He pointed his empty beer bottle in my face. "Alright, but remember that's what you want," he said, then walked out, letting the screen door slam behind him.

I had to relax, calm myself down before I exploded and went on a rampage. As an alternative, I changed clothes and took Bruiser for a walk down to Boathouse Row. It was a warm, seventy-degree night, so Kelly Drive was crowded with other casual strollers as well as serious joggers and bikers. My thoughts turned to my sister. Did I have enough nerve to ask her about the test results? Why had she looked so bad on Memorial Day? Could she really be hurting as bad as I was?

When I returned to the house I ran a tub of water and got in before it was full and covered my face with the washcloth to soak up my tears. I couldn't believe I'd let one conversation with Malik bring me to tears. Rather than listen to my thoughts I turned up the CD player and let Beyoncé remind me that all I had was "Me, Myself, and I."

Lying there I allowed myself to think about G-dog. He was no replacement for Malik; however, he kept me from being lonely. I was only with him because he was around when I'd begun to fall into the abyss that was now my life. But I was determined to pull myself out.

The last thing I had to clean up was the two carats that remained on my left ring finger. Despite my anger at Malik's betrayal, I'd kept the ring on because I truly loved him. Sitting on the edge of the bed, I tugged at the ring, and when it wouldn't slide off easily, I spread lotion between my fingers until it began to rise over my knuckle. I'd been so excited when Malik surprised me with the ring. We'd been on a weekend getaway at a bed-and-breakfast on Lake George and were out to dinner when he'd proposed. Down on one knee and everything—the stuff I only thought happened in fairy tales. I guess that my cynicism had proved to be true, because this relationship definitely didn't have a happy ending.

There was no denying I missed the closeness of my family. I wondered if Kamille had found out anything in her search for her biological parents or if she'd had any luck getting a new job. She hated working at the parking authority with all its politics and had been applying for work in the private sector. We'd revised her résumé before all this happened and I had no idea what was presently going on with her. Maybe I still did care about my sister.

Kamille had always completed me. She'd always had the better ideas. It was just that I implemented them. And now I was without her.

Rather than risk calling her and not knowing what to say, I called my parents and apologized for my behavior on Memorial Day.

"Mom . . ." I could barely get her name out before I started crying.

"Tiffany, is that you? Now, come on, honey. It's alright, you don't have to cry."

"But, Mom, I was wrong. I should've never acted like that. It was just that I was so mixed up."

"I know. Now, stop that crying."

"But what about Dad? Is he still mad at me?"

"Of course not. We just want you and your sister to make up, okay?"

"We will, Mom. I promise."

The next call I made was to my brother, Julian. According to my mother he had been pulled up from the minor leagues to play for the Boston Red Sox when their shortstop had been injured. I just hoped he didn't turn into one of those athletes with nasty attitudes that my boss Sasha used to represent. He didn't answer, so I left him a message telling him I loved him and that I was going to call Kamille this week and talk with her.

For the first time in a while I slept soundly that night, knowing that my future would be brighter once I talked with my sister. Even if Malik was Kareem's father, it wasn't worth losing my sister over.

While half watching the news the next morning I caught the end of a press conference in which district attorney Gregory Haney discussed the results of an overnight drug sting operation his office had conducted.

". . . indictments of eleven individuals for their involvement in an international drug ring specializing in the importation and distribution of methamphetamine and the club drug known as Ecstasy. My intentions are to put a stranglehold on this epidemic."

I noticed he was extremely well groomed, dressed in a navy blue, double-breasted suit, with a crisp white shirt and bold red-and-blue striped tie. Looking at him closely, I realized he was more handsome than I remembered. I could see where

G-dog inherited his pretty boy looks. Even though Mr. Haney was married, it was easy to see how a man of his looks had gained the reputation of a ladies' man. His smooth, commanding voice and confident demeanor were almost mesmerizing. I doubted if G-dog would ever be that polished. Sitting on the edge of the bed, I continued to listen.

". . . Five of those persons were running drugs between New York and Florida. In the last twenty-four hours we've seized a large shipment of cocaine, which included fifty thousand tablets of Ecstasy with an approximate street value of $5.3 million. Additional court-authorized search warrants will be executed . . ."

I thought about how Mr. Haney had said he was proud that I was part of his family. I began to fantasize about meeting him, how I would dress, what I would say. My musings about Mr. Haney were interrupted when the phone rang.

"Hey, I got your message last night. Check this out. I made some calls and now your permits are ready. But I'm at a rec center out in Tacony and won't be able to pick them up in time."

"G-dog, I really need them. I have to get them over to the contractor by today or they're gonna have to stop work. And I damn sure don't want any construction delays, especially since I'm still paying while they're not working."

"Yeah, yeah, I know. So this is what I need you to do. Call my dad at his office and you can go by there and pick them up."

"G-dog, I can't do that. I mean, I haven't even met your father yet."

"Naw, it's cool. I just talked to him and told him you'd come get 'em. Just call him and let him know what time you'll be there to pick them up."

"I guess I don't have a choice then. Alright, what's the number?"

I phoned the DA's office and was told by his appointment secretary that she'd give him my message when he returned from the mayor's office. I couldn't believe I'd been fantasizing about meeting Mr. Haney only minutes before and now I actually would! My pulse quickened as I slipped into a chartreuse halter dress, and to take it up a notch, I went without a bra.

After running some errands and treating myself to lunch at the Continental, I made it to the club by two o'clock. The Eighteenth Street steps leading to Teaz were stained with paint and debris. There was a large Dumpster in the yard beside it. Inside the building the previous wall and ceiling coverings had been stripped and the construction workers had just completed hanging Sheetrock. I could smell the joint compound they'd applied. Maybe things were coming together after all.

I was just beginning to explain to Frank, the contractor, that I'd have the permits later that day when my cell phone rang.

"Good afternoon. Tiffany Johnson, please."

I recognized Mr. Haney's voice from the news that morning. "Oh, hello, Mr. Haney. G-dog, I mean, your son said I could call you to come pick up the permits."

"Yes, but I'm on my way out. Is there someplace I could drop them off to you?" Mr. Haney's voice was low-pitched, just like on television.

"Well, I'm at Teaz right now. I mean the club. You could have someone drop them off here if you'd like."

"It's not a problem. I'll bring them myself. I've heard so much about you from my son that I'm looking forward to meeting you. You're at Eighteenth and Walnut, right?"

"Yes," I said, but what I really wanted to ask was why he'd taken it upon himself to talk about me to Malik.

"Okay, you should see me in about an hour."

By 5:30 the workers had left and Mr. Haney still hadn't shown up. I didn't want to call his office, so I decided I'd leave and just wait to hear from him. I was locking up the front door when I saw him pull up in a black Mercedes. Leaving the door open, I stepped inside to switch on the lights.

When I turned to walk back to the door I was startled to find Mr. Haney standing directly behind me.

"I'm sorry. Did I scare you?" he asked.

"No, I saw you parking but I didn't hear you come in."

He extended his hand and said, "It's a pleasure to meet you, Tiffany Johnson."

When I reached out to shake his hand he turned mine over and kissed my palm.

"The pleasure is all mine, Mr. Haney," I said, enjoying the feel of his warm lips against my palm.

I was a little nervous because I hadn't expected his presence to be so powerful.

"What's taken us so long to meet?"

"I've just been busy, but I told your son I was looking forward to meeting you and your wife as well."

His eyes took in my dress and stopped on my cleavage. Maybe not wearing a bra had been a bad idea.

"You are truly a black beauty, just like my son describes you."

"Oh, really. Is that how G-dog refers to me?"

He laughed, and then looked around the trash-strewn room. "It looks like you have a long way to go here."

"Not really. They'll start painting tomorrow."

"Does that mean you don't have anything to drink in this place?"

"No, but we're not supposed to open the boxes until we get our liquor license."

"Well, then, I guess you're in luck. I have it and the others right here."

I went to the storage closet and tried to rip open one of the boxes marked Smirnoff.

"Here, let me do it."

While he pried open the box I went to answer my ringing cell phone. I told him where he could find some cups. The call was from Essence, reminding me that we had several interviews lined up at the club the next morning.

When I went back to Mr. Haney I noticed he'd already poured our drinks. He passed one of the paper cups to me. I tried to see which bottle he'd opened but he'd already replaced it in the box.

"This is good," I said. "What did you mix?"

"Just a little blend I use. Now tell me, when does this place officially open?"

"Friday before Labor Day, if all goes as planned."

He finished his drink and poured another. "You want one?"

"Why not?" I answered, surprised to find myself drinking alone with G-dog's father. I was beginning to feel a little more relaxed, so maybe one more drink wouldn't hurt. I held my cup out for a refill.

"Here, sit down," he said, moving empty soda cans from the top of a large container of joint compound. "Looks like you need to take a load off," he commented, glancing down as I crossed my legs before pouring my drink.

"Here you go."

"Thanks."

"Now, besides the permits, is there anything else I can do for the lovely Tiffany Johnson, because you seem a little tense."

"No, everything is fine."

"How are things with you and my son? There's not going to be a problem with your Mr. Skinner, is there?"

"Of course not. I'm not seeing Mr. Skinner anymore," I answered quickly. Malik was the last person I wanted to talk about right then.

"That would be a good thing. You know, Tiffany, my son is a good kid though he rarely takes interest in anything for too long, especially women. Which means there must be something special about you."

Why was he telling me all this? I wasn't planning a future with his son. More importantly, I liked the way Mr. Haney was looking at me, and the way I was beginning to feel, which was horny.

"But G-dog, as you call him, knows a good investment when he sees one," Mr. Haney said with a smile.

"Are you saying I'm one of his investments?"

Rather than answer, he sipped his drink, then loosened his tie, his eyes on me the entire time.

I stood up. "I think I need to get going. I have to be back here early tomorrow."

"Aww, come now. It's not often I get to share a drink with a sexy woman like yourself."

As I tried to get out of his way, he put his hand on my lower back. I looked up at him and our eyes met and held.

"You know, Mr. Hane . . . I . . . I . . . I don't think . . ." I couldn't quite get my words together. What the hell was wrong with me? This man had a strange power over me.

"What is it, dear?" he asked, but now he was so close I could smell his aftershave. It didn't help that the heat from the closed-up club was stifling, making beads of sweat form between my breasts. He leaned down and kissed me, first gently, then deeply. He held me in his strong arms and I felt myself melting.

Without warning a wave of dizziness came over me. I backed away and used my hand to fan myself, as I was starting to really feel the effects of everything I'd been drinking. Mr. Haney asked what was wrong with me, as he held my face in his hands and looked at me with concern. I shook my head and said, "Really, nothing. Just the fumes in here and the drink. Maybe we should open a window."

"Or, maybe this would help," he said, taking a small bottle of pills out of his pocket.

"What do you have there?" I asked.

"Just something I take when I need a little boost." He massaged my neck and shoulders, and then held my hand and began massaging it.

I sighed deeply and began to feel better. I started to abandon myself to the seductive way he massaged me, finding all the tight points and loosening them, nibbling and kissing and licking my hand. I closed my eyes and gave in to the sensations. That's when he put the little pill in my palm.

I opened my eyes. "What did you say this was?"

"It's Ecstasy," he said. "Just a little something to get you feeling good if you're tense or tired. It won't hurt you." He kissed me again, a long, deep, powerful kiss that had my head reeling. I kissed him back and as I felt an irresistible hunger for him growing inside me, I wrapped my legs around him. He took the pill out of my hand and brought it to my lips.

He kissed me on the forehead and placed his hand behind my head, cradling it. I looked up into his eyes and took the pill onto the tip of my tongue, licking his finger as I did so. He held my drink up to my lips while I swallowed a sip to wash it down.

"You okay?" Mr. Haney's closeness felt good, as did the feel of his hands as he rubbed them up and down my thighs. My body began to tingle. His muscular thighs squeezed tighter against mine as we kissed again.

"My God, Tiffany. You're so damn black and so beautiful. Do you always dress so sexy?"

I could hear Mr. Haney talking, but he sounded far away. Somewhere in my head I had thoughts of G-dog and Malik, but the thoughts were too faint for me to pay attention. Focusing my eyes on the exit door, I realized my vision was fuzzy. Could I be that drunk? I'd only had two drinks, I thought. It must be the Ecstasy making me feel this way. While he stepped back to look at me I turned around and began to climb the ladder leaning against the wall nearby. Realizing I was going nowhere, I tried to step back down, but his hands gripped the sides of the ladder while his mouth gently bit the cheeks of my ass.

My pussy was beginning to pulsate even though I knew what we were doing wasn't right. He was G-dog's father.

Almost as if he'd heard my thoughts, he lifted my dress and slid my panties down. I looked to my right and could see my knuckles turning red as I held tightly to the sides of the ladder. This wasn't right. It couldn't be right. Maybe I was home drunk and dreaming. Hadn't I seen Mr. Haney on television just that morning?

I began to ask him to stop, but he wrapped my hair that hung loose down my back around his hands and tilted my head back. With his face buried under my dress, his tongue gently tickled the place where Malik's had never gone. He ran his tongue up and down the crack of my ass while I lay weak and helpless against the ladder. Without wanting to, I cried out for him to fuck me because I knew that there was no stopping what had already begun to unfold. I had to have Mr. Haney.

Gently he pried my hands loose from the ladder and turned me around to face him. He gently brushed the back of his hand across my face, bringing with it a tingling sensation that rippled its way from my toes up through my body, hardening my nipples. Why was I so horny? I wanted to say something but my mouth was too dry. Mr. Haney must have sensed my thirst because he handed me the warm cup of alcohol. I sipped, then placed my mouth over his, causing the liquid to spill from my lips to his.

Reaching under my knee, he hoisted my leg and placed it on top of the joint compound can where I'd sat, and with his other hand he pushed his fingers inside me. My body immediately let loose a gush of fluids. I quickly found his zipper, unbuckled his belt, and let his pants fall to the floor.

When his dick sprung from the opening of his boxers I heard him snicker, probably at the surprised look on my face when I saw how long and thick it was. Mr. Haney was going to do it to me so good, I told myself, much better than his son. But shouldn't I have been fighting him off?

"I can't let you do this to me, please, I never . . ."

Without taking his eyes from me, he nodded as if he understood. "You're going to let me fuck you. Aren't you, lovely lady?" he asked, while brushing my hair out of my face. I pulled his hand to my mouth and kissed his fingers. He in turn brought his lips down over mine. It was like I'd never been kissed before. Our mouths became one, or so I thought, as his tongue chased itself around mine.

"Mis . . . ter . . . uh, Mister. Hane . . ." I mumbled, my mouth moving to his neck.

He responded by gently tugging on my nipples with his teeth. I wiggled underneath him in a final attempt to get away, but my body was on fire for Mr. Haney like it had never been for anyone.

"I think you're almost ready, lovely lady. Now, let me see." And with that his fingers touched the juices that had gathered between my thighs. Placing them under his nose, he closed his eyes and sniffed, taking in their smell before easing them inside me. Every nerve in my body danced. Whatever he'd done to make me feel this way, I wanted him to do it again and again.

He reached down, dipped his thick forefinger far inside my pussy, then rubbed it across my lips as he gradually pushed himself inside me. I'd never been with somebody so big, and if he hadn't been so gentle with me I was sure he could've ripped my insides open. Rather than begin to fuck me, he just let it sit in there, and when I started to move he told me to wait.

Slowly, he worked his way inside, loosening up my walls to make room for him. I couldn't get enough, so he used his hands and lifted my petite body off the floor. I wrapped my legs around his back.

Just when I thought I'd taken it all in, he pulled himself from me. I gasped from the emptiness his dick left behind.

"Please don't take it out."

"Come on, let me give it to you right," he said, stroking himself so I could see how my juices had glazed his dick. He put his hands on my shoulders and guided me down to my knees. I knew how dirty the floor was but at that moment I didn't care. So there I kneeled between empty soda cans and cigarette butts and took Mr. Haney's long, thick dick in my mouth, flicking my tongue around its head, making it wet with my saliva.

"Whew, you're such a good . . . ahhhh . . . how'd you . . ."

I worked hard because I wanted to please him, and he responded by twisting my hair around his hands and pushing himself deeper into the back of my throat. Looking up, my eyes met his, and when I leaned back to catch my breath he reached for his dick and slapped me across the face with it. I was surprised to feel my pleasure center drip in response.

"Suck my dick, you pretty black bitch," he commanded, using it to slap me again.

I took him deeper into my mouth this time, maneuvering his large dick until I was comfortable. I worked it in and out until I could feel it pulsating. I had one hand on his balls and the other I used to rub my clit. I was ready to come, but he pulled away.

He picked me up and kissed me hungrily like he loved me, like he missed me, then he led me over to a drop cloth that lay crumpled on the floor. I lay on my back for him, spreading my legs open.

"Good girl," he said.

I watched as Mr. Haney removed the rest of his clothes and tossed them on a bar stool. I closed my eyes and waited for him to come to me, but instead of his heated body I felt a cold and creamy texture being rubbed across my breasts. When I opened my eyes I saw that he was smearing gray joint compound over my body.

"I'm going to take good care of you, Tiffany Johnson," he said, while situating my legs on his shoulders and thrusting his dick so far up into me that I thought I'd peed myself. I tried to slow him down and crawl away but he smacked me on my ass.

"Where do you think you're going? Hold your ass still while I give you this dick," he commanded in a gruff voice.

Tears welled up in my eyes, as much from pain as from pleasure. He ignored me and continued to use his hands as a weapon on my ass, repeatedly smacking me until fluid ran so thick down my thighs that I thought something had broke inside of me from his strange method of lovemaking. But my climax didn't stop him.

My body was limp and I could barely lift my head to look up at him to figure out what he wanted me to do. Mr. Haney didn't give me much time to think of anything because he was now forcing me to turn over and up on my elbows and knees.

"Please, please, it's too big. I won't be able to take it like this," I cried to him.

Kneeling behind me he used his hands to spread my cheeks and then began easing every inch of his long dick back inside me, causing my trembling body to collapse from yet another orgasm. Mr. Haney was unstoppable, and maybe his sex drive was unquenchable, too. I began to feel like this night might never end.

Eventually he had his fill of me, and I of him. It was probably well after midnight when I turned off the lights and crept out of the building.

5

ON THE WAGON

The next morning I awoke from what must've been a coma. My limbs felt like fifty-pound weights, making it impossible for me to even sit up. My throat was dry, and my mouth so parched that it hurt when I tried to open it. What the hell had happened? And then it all came back to me. Mr. Haney, the permits, drinking at the club, the white pill I'd swallowed. My God, what had I done?

I struggled to get out of bed, where I'd obviously slept in my clothes. My thighs felt like rubber and the space between my legs was numb. My body ached to the point that I could only move in slow motion. But the worst part was the stomach cramps and nausea.

So I lay back down and tried to piece it together. There

had to be some rationale for my behavior. Had I actually been that drunk, or worse, that horny? I desperately wanted to fall back into another deep sleep and forget Mr. Haney, but when I checked the messages on my voice mail I realized I was already late for my meeting at the club with Essence.

When I arrived at Teaz two hours later it was obvious that Essence was irritated.

"What the hell did you do last night? I thought you were going to chill out from that drinking and shit. Frank says somebody left the place unlocked last night."

I tried not to look in her face as I made my way to the makeshift office on one side of the room, which consisted of a few chairs and an old desk.

"Look at yourself, Tiffany. Your hands are shaking. You're burnt the hell out, and let's not even talk about what's going on with your sister."

"I'm just tired, that's all," I said, knowing I was guilty. I had forgotten to phone Kamille. "Can we just get this over with, okay? And believe me, Essence, this isn't the time to discuss Kamille. I've already made the decision to talk to her, if that makes you feel any better."

I looked around the room to see if there was any evidence of my tryst with Mr. Haney. Nothing had changed from last night. Empty soda cans, paint buckets, and the drop cloth were still on the floor. It was just that now most of it had been swept up into a pile.

I listened as Essence and Jeff, our director of operations, interviewed barmaids, coat check girls, and managers. I drank bottle after bottle of water because my throat was so dry. Just as

I was beginning to come around, the contractor walked over and asked me for the permits. The room seemed to go silent as I dug through my purse for those two brown envelopes.

After a few more agonizing moments of searching my purse, I was able to say, "Umm, yeah. They're right here," and pull the envelopes out. He took them from my hand and walked away.

Relieved, I reached for a bottle of water.

Looking at my hand, Essence asked, "What's that shit under your nails?"

When I looked down to see what she was referring to, I noticed the joint compound still stuck there. I excused myself and went into the bathroom where, try as I might, the dried plaster just wouldn't go away.

I had to get out of there and go home, but we had two more people to interview. As I tried to muddle through my thoughts and pull myself together, I paid no attention to the people being interviewed until the last candidate arrived.

Leila was boyishly beautiful with short hair and a carefully sculpted body, but there was no mistaking she was a woman. She wore a pair of black low-rise pants and a pale yellow shirt that showed just a peek of what appeared to be a strawberry tattoo on her stomach.

"Good afta-noon," she said, in a clipped accent.

Essence greeted her but with some distaste. Leila told us she was Filipino and black when Essence asked what nationality gave her the slight accent. I let Essence begin interviewing Leila for the bar manager position as I reviewed her résumé. Seeing that she'd worked as a club manager in London, Vegas, and most recently the Hamptons, I was already impressed. I stole glances at her while she spoke with Essence, who was trying to figure out where they'd met before. I assumed from the tone of the conversation that Leila, too, was bisexual. When I looked up from her résumé my gaze met Leila's.

"Leila, how long have you been in Philly?"

"Just a few weeks, but I've been looking to meet you, Tiffany."

"Thanks," I said, lowering my head, embarrassed that she'd caught me staring at her.

"Well, your résumé is definitely impressive," I said.

"Thank you."

After the interview concluded I shared my observations with Essence. "She is nice, smart, and experienced. I think we should hire her."

"What are you talking about? Just because she's a gorgeous dyke doesn't mean she can do the job. Anyway, you barely said two words."

"I know, but I was listening."

"Well, I don't know. I realized where I've seen her. She hangs out at Meow Mix in New York."

"Stop being jealous and hire the woman," I said, then stepped outside for fresh air before Essence could respond.

By the time we wrapped up it was 5:00 P.M. I wanted desperately to tell Essence about what had happened with Mr. Haney, but she was rushing off to Washington, D.C., to do a guest DJ spot, so she didn't have time to talk.

I knew I had to talk to someone, and when it came down to it Kamille was the only one outside of Essence whom I could think of to trust. As I pulled out of the parking lot next to Teaz my cell phone rang. It was G-dog. I panicked—what would I say to him? Had his father told him already?

I flipped the phone open. "Hello? G-dog?"

"Yo, girl. Where you at? You get the permits?"

Why did he try to talk so damn cool? It was beginning to get on my nerves. All of a sudden I didn't like him anymore.

"I'm just about to leave the club."

"You want me to swing by there?"

"No, no, don't do that. I'm on my way to Kamille's house."

"Damn, when did all that happen? I guess you made up with that nigga, too."

"G-dog, look, I don't have time for this right now. I'll have to call you back." Without waiting for his response, I dropped the phone into my purse.

It rang again and this time it was Mr. Haney. What did he want?

"Well, black beauty, I see you've recovered from last night. I must say you really do know how to satisfy a man."

"Mr. Haney, I'm begging you not to tell G-dog what happened. I don't know what was wrong with me."

"Your secret is safe with me."

"I don't want us to have a secret. I mean, I do, but this can't ever happen again. You understand?"

"But what if you need me, lovely lady?"

"I doubt that very much. Just please stay away from me."

"You can't be serious about that, especially since you were craving what I gave you."

I couldn't believe I was having this conversation with the district attorney, G-dog's father. I ended the call.

But Mr. Haney was right. I'd never had that many orgasms with any man, and for once I didn't have to take control. I had wanted to try something kinky with Malik, but nothing as outrageous as what I experienced with Mr. Haney.

I pulled out of the parking lot and, without really planning to, drove to my sister's house in Queen Village.

While maneuvering my truck into a parking space on Snyder Avenue, I caught a glimpse of a familiar car in my rearview mirror. I didn't think much of it until I saw the lady of justice figure dangling from the mirror. It was Malik's silver Volvo.

Leaving the engine running, I opened the door and jumped out of my truck, almost getting hit by a passing motorist. Falling back against the truck, I held my hands to my chest in hopes of stopping its awful pounding. Why was Malik there? Maybe he and my sister were back together. But how could they explain it to my nephews? Tears choked my throat as I tried to will myself to walk across the street to confront them.

I was contemplating knocking on the door and listening to what they had to say. But what if they didn't want to talk to me anymore? I took a few steps away from the idling truck, then hesitated again, leaning back against the truck door, slamming it shut.

I had to get back in the truck before anybody saw me. I tried to open the Navigator's door but it was locked. Stricken with panic, I looked up and down the street, hoping no one had spotted me yet. I wondered if Malik still had my truck keys on his key ring. Banging my head against the window, I tried to think of what to do. If I left the truck running someone would probably steal it, and if I took the time to call AAA, then Malik would know I'd been here. I heard the ringing of a phone and looked down at my waist pouch. Suddenly I remembered that it held my spare key.

As I unlocked the truck door I realized that I needed to take action. Why was I running from them? If they were having another affair, I couldn't let them get off so easy. Not this time. I made my way across the street, up my sister's steps, and banged on her door. Malik answered.

"What the hell are you doing here?" I asked him.

"Why don't you ask your sister. She's right here," he said, gesturing toward the living room.

I looked over at the couch, where Kamille sat bopping her head to the loud music video playing on her television.

"Look who it is. Ms. High and Mighty has finally showed up. What do you want?"

This didn't sound like my sister. Why was she being so arrogant?

"Where are my nephews?" I asked the both of them.

"Your parents took the boys to Boston to visit your brother," Malik informed me.

"And that's why you're here? Please tell me you found out something."

"Talk to your sister. I've had enough, and it looks to me like you two deserve each other." Malik headed out the front door.

"Kamille, what the hell is wrong with you? Are you high on something?"

"Like you give a damn. All you wanna know is who my baby's daddy is." She laughed to herself.

"Kamille, stop this right now and tell me why you're acting like this."

"Me? You're the one who kicked me out your life and didn't care how nobody felt but yourself, so why do you care now?"

She walked over to the dining room table and poured herself a drink of Hennessy. When had Kamille started drinking so much? Hadn't she been the one who said that too much drinking ruined a light-skinned girl's complexion?

"You know what—to hell with you, Kamille. Suit yourself if you want to sit here and get stoned out of your mind. When you're ready to talk, you call me."

"Fuck you, Tiffany. You ain't shit either."

When I walked out the door I could hear her laughing behind my back. I guess she was amused because now the joke was on me. I was ready to talk and she couldn't have cared less.

As I left my sister's house all I could think about was getting drunk myself. I had to go somewhere and get myself together before I exploded into tiny pieces. At Second Street, I pulled up outside of Lounge OneTwoFive. I didn't have the patience to park, so I handed my keys to the valet.

It was too crowded to get a seat at the bar, so I found a spot in one of their intimate living-room areas. Alone, drinking a Sapphire and tonic, I still couldn't get out of my mind the mess I'd made of things.

I was proceeding to get drunk when I saw Leila come in. I watched her flit around the club, laughing and talking carefree with people. She really was beautiful. I didn't feel like talking to her so I lowered my head, trying not to be noticed. I started reassuring myself that getting drunk would make me forget everything. Just as I was about to call G-dog to join me on my binge, I felt someone touch my shoulder.

"Tiffany, why are you sitting here by yourself? Is everything alright?" Leila asked.

"Who, me? I just stopped by for a drink before I head home. I was down at the club all afternoon," I said, in defense of my drinking in solitude. "What are you doing here?"

"Looking for you," she joked, and then sat down on the round steel table in front of me.

"Yeah, right," I answered, as I absentmindedly nibbled on peanuts from the bowl beside me.

Leila made me uncomfortable for so many reasons; she exuded too much sexuality and her dark eyes seemed to pierce through the wall I was trying to put up.

"Actually, I'm supposed to be meeting someone, but I don't see her yet," she said, glancing behind her toward the entrance.

"I see. So, are you working somewhere in town?"

Her confused expression made me feel stupid for asking. Wasn't she just at Teaz that morning, applying for a job?

"I'm hoping to get the chance to work with you, Tiffany."

"Yeah, I hope so, too."

Her face brightened up, so I assumed that whomever she

was waiting for must've come through the door. Her date was a young woman, I'm sure no more than twenty-two, dressed in a short dress that barely covered her ass and three-inch high-heeled sandals. She waved to Leila and scurried over to us, bending over to kiss Leila on the mouth.

Leila introduced us, and the woman's response to meeting me made me want to disappear.

"Hi, how are you?" I said, forgetting her name that quickly.

"*You're* Tiffany?" she asked, seeming surprised.

"Yep, that's me," I answered, looking up at her. She stood over Leila, her sculpted nails resting on Leila's shoulder.

"Wow, you're not exactly like what I thought," she said, turning her head from Leila to me as if questioning who I really was.

Embarrassed at however bad I was looking, I averted my eyes and instead looked down into my now watery drink.

"Oh, I'm sorry. I just expected . . . I dunno," she said, trying to apologize.

"Come on, girl. Let's go," Leila said, realizing that my feelings had been hurt. "Tiffany, I'll holla at you later."

My night now ruined, I fished a twenty out my purse and handed it to my waitress. I took the elevator to the first floor and recovered my car, barely speaking to acquaintances who called out to me.

After arriving home I gave myself a once-over in my bedroom's full-length mirror. My face looked tired, and worry lines were furrowing my brow, trying to find a permanent home. My eyes were red and glaring, my hair limp and in need of a perm and a trim after being in a ponytail for a month. My jeans felt tight, as if I'd gained a few pounds from drinking and endless take-out meals. No wonder Leila's friend was surprised at what I looked like. My reflection was void of color and life, just like I felt inside.

This summer was proving to be a series of drunken binges for me. And from the looks of my sister tonight, she, too, was having a rough time of it. She and Malik had been right. I had been selfish to think that I was the only one suffering. I wasn't sure if I could ease their pain, but I was determined to ease my own. I told myself that I could make things right. The fact that I'd hooked up with G-dog's father coupled with my broken relationships with Malik and Kamille had sent me over the edge. I knew I wasn't doing myself any good with my downward spiral and I was determined to put a stop to it.

There was no ignoring Bruiser's need to go out. I knew he was tired of being caged up in the house all the time with his only exercise being when I let him out in the backyard. Yawning, Bruiser looked up at me and whined. I was tired of whining and crying to myself about all the things that were wrong in my life.

I went to the kitchen, found his leash, and clipped it onto the rhinestone collar I'd bought him, and we headed toward Kelly Drive for a walk. From now on I would be fully focused on Teaz.

6

DOG DAYS OF SUMMER

I found that the best way to push my tryst with Mr. Haney and the infidelity of Kamille and Malik from my mind was to fill every minute of my day with preparations for the grand opening of Teaz. It was only a few short weeks away, so it was time for us to pick out fabrics, chairs, glassware, and all the other fine details that would make the place exceptional. I spent a lot of time with the public relations company we'd hired to ensure that we'd have celebrities for the grand opening and that everyone was aware of Teaz's existence. Even with my own contacts, I was glad to have the assistance.

By now Essence and I had hired two additional managers and a staff of thirty employees. We'd also brought Leila on board. I couldn't help but wonder if I would have fallen straight to my demise if I hadn't run into her and her girlfriend that night at OneTwoFive. I wanted to thank Leila, so I was glad when she called my office one afternoon to suggest I stop by her apartment for lunch. It was a much needed break, to say the least.

Rather than drive and deal with trying to find a parking space, I hopped a cab to her place at Second and Brown in the new and trendy neighborhood of Bella Vista. Her loft was on the second floor of an old clothing factory. I had to ride a rickety elevator that I was sure hadn't been inspected in years.

A well-tanned Leila answered the door in a pair of paint-stained sweat shorts that hung low on her hips. Her waist was adorned with a gold belly chain and her nipples protruded from her shredded T-shirt.

"Leila, thanks for the invite."

"Tiffany, girl, you look hot!"

"I do? Thanks. I mean, I do feel better."

She placed a friendly kiss on my lips. "What are you wearing? You smell delicious. You know, I'm sorry if my girlfriend offended you down at OneTwoFive."

"It's alright. It was exactly what I needed to hear to shake the funk I've been in," I said, as she ushered me through the wide doorway.

"I don't wanna get into your business, but is everything okay?"

"Yeah, it's all good and it'll be even better once we open the doors of Teaz."

As I walked through Leila's loft, I could see it was full of things she loved. Despite the lack of an air conditioner, the air inside was cooled by the breeze created by five antique ceiling fans located throughout the large space. At one end of the loft was an island kitchen adjacent to a black oblong table with six mismatched chairs. At the other end of her loft was her king-size bed, which sat on a raised platform, and behind it large industrial windows served as a head-board. But what really caught my eye were the photographs along the walls.

"Leila, these are breathtaking," I commented, admiring the beautiful oversized photographs of women that covered her walls. "Did you take all these?"

The photos were mostly of naked women, and those of stylized female body parts were in black and white. By her bed was a Georgia O'Keeffe print whose flowers always reminded me of vaginas.

"Yes. I've been doing these for a long time. Hey, you should let me shoot you one day. I bet you'd look beautiful on my wall."

"Well, give me a few more months and maybe then I can look as good as these women," I said, pointing at a portrait of a woman's naked behind.

"Tiffany, you've always looked gorgeous to me, and those eyes, girl. Whew!"

"Thanks, Leila."

I sat down at the table and saw she'd made a Caesar salad with grilled shrimp and a pitcher of fresh lemonade. I watched her setting the table and wondered what she actually did when she had a woman in bed.

"Now, tell me, Leila how'd you land in Philly from all those great places you listed on your résumé?"

"Simply got tired of moving around all the time, looking for the right job, right woman. I have an old friend here in Philly who told me about your place and I decided to see if I could get on board."

"I'm so glad you're with us. I think Teaz is really going to put Philly on the map again. I've already started getting calls from people wanting to make reservations for private parties, and all they've seen is the website."

"You really do look good, Tiffany. There's something I must do. Wait right here."

Leila crossed the room to her closet, and when she emerged she began snapping my picture. I feigned embarrassment by covering my face with my hands.

"C'mon, now. All women want to look beautiful for the camera," she said, pulling my hands down from my face.

"Are you always this spontaneous?"

Moving in close, she took another shot.

"I know beauty when I see it. Now, give me a sexy one."

I laughed, then flashed her my breasts, and she snapped another one. Before I knew it Leila had snapped an entire roll of film.

While we ate Leila admitted that she knew Essence didn't particularly care for her and understood when I told her that Essence was just being overprotective of me.

"That's just because she thinks I'm going to try to lure you into bed."

"You're bi, too?" I asked, averting my eyes to search my salad. I forked a grape tomato and put it in my mouth.

"Hell no. I'm all about women. Leila don't want no parts of a man when it comes to love."

"Is it easy to pick up women?"

"I picked you up, didn't I," she answered, laughing at the embarrassed look on my face.

I cracked up, too. I guess she had picked me up, because besides Teaz we probably didn't have much in common.

"But seriously though, straight women always think we're desperate to sleep with anybody, when in reality for me it's gotta be more than just a hole with some hair on it. I have to feel some passion."

"Wow, passion, huh. Between two women."

"C'mon, Tiff. You mean you've never been even a little curious?"

"Actually, no."

She laughed at that, probably not believing me. "Tiffany, every woman has been curious or we wouldn't be having this conversation."

"Is it that easy to tell?"

She leaned across the table toward me, allowing me to see deep into her cleavage. I could see the heaving of her breasts, which reminded me of the woman in the bathroom at Pousse.

"It's like this. If I flirt with a woman who's curious, she has a different way of responding—she gets it."

"I see," I said.

Feeling a little uneasy discussing Leila's sexuality, I changed the subject by telling her about the house I'd seen in the Hamptons. I'd been thinking about it lately but had been putting off going back up there by telling myself that I'd probably never have any time to spend there. This seemed to get her excited.

"The Hamptons are beautiful, Tiffany. I've been there a lot. You should grab that place up. I mean, how bad could it be? Once you get it I guarantee you'll go up there every chance you get. You'll probably end up wanting to buy it."

"I don't know. It might not be worth the money. It looked like it needed a lotta work."

"Stop being so negative and at least call the realtor and see what they want for it."

"You're right. What have I got to lose?"

She was insistent that I call the realtor that afternoon from her apartment and actually put her cordless phone in my hand so I could make the call. I retrieved the number from my PalmPilot and within a few hours, I'd rented the cottage in the Hamptons.

However, my new turn on things didn't make G-dog too happy. It meant I didn't have time for him, or at least that's how I made it seem. I just couldn't bear the guilt of looking in his face after what had happened with his father. I almost felt as if I had to apologize to him for something he knew nothing about. But my guilt didn't keep me from thinking back on the pleasure I experienced that night with Mr. Haney. I doubted that I could ever forget, and I'd come to the conclusion that he didn't want our secret to be exposed either. To make up for my absence and not cause any suspicion, I agreed to hang out with G-dog at the Wooden Iron bar in Wayne. It was far enough from the city that I didn't have to really socialize with anybody I knew, or run into my sister again.

As we made our way through the crowded bar filled with young preppies, probably my age and younger, similar to the crowd from the Hamptons, G-dog stopped to speak to just about everyone. It was almost as if he were holding court. The people he introduced me to had heard about Teaz and couldn't wait to come into the city to hang out at the club. G-dog was so busy socializing with people in the restaurant and talking on his cell phone that he barely paid me any attention. Hell, if he hadn't been the DA's son, I would've taken him for a drug dealer.

As I watched G-dog work the bar I noticed some of the mannerisms he shared with his father—the way he held his hands and the smirk that most times covered his face. It was a little too unnerving for me, so while he sat on a bar stool bragging about some deal he'd made, I excused myself and went to the ladies' room. Just as I was about to return to my seat a young white guy stepped in front of me to speak to G-dog. When G-dog raised his arm to shake his hand, I noticed a bulge at his side. Why the hell was G-dog carrying a gun?

For the first time I became suspicious of G-dog's activities, so I kept my eyes on him to see if he was passing anything to anyone that resembled a package containing drugs. But he came away clean each time. Concentrating on him was making me feel ridiculous, so rather than continue to guess why G-dog was carrying a gun, and if the reason he had the attention of all these kids was because he was dealing drugs, I confronted him about it.

"Why are you carrying this?" I asked, my hand on the steel piece he had strapped to his side.

"What? This?" he asked, touching the gun. "My father's been getting some threats and he wanted me to protect myself."

"You're not selling drugs, are you?"

"Girl, are you crazy? Why would I do some shit like that?" he said, and then kissed me.

"I mean, all these people out here and in Philly . . . it doesn't look right."

He placed his hands on my shoulders, bringing me close to him. "Tiffany, baby, now you and I both know"—he lowered his voice before continuing—"that I play this little game of being part street politician and part bad guy."

"Why do you do that, anyway?"

"It's all for my father. These are the people who vote, and if they vote for G-dog, they'll vote for my father." All the time he was reassuring me, he kept one eye on the crowd. He noticed a group of people entering the bar and excused himself. "I need to talk to some people for a minute. I'll be outside. But I want you to make a run with me down to my folks' house."

Before I could say hell no, he'd walked away, leaving me standing there with my mouth open. I followed him outside and came up with every excuse imaginable as to why I couldn't go to his parents' house. Finally, a querying look came over his face.

"What the hell is wrong with you? I've been seeing you for months and you don't want to meet my parents? I mean, you met my father already, so what gives?"

There was no way I could tell him the truth, so finally I agreed to go. I was a nervous wreck all the way back into the city worrying about how I should act, what I should say. The worst part was wondering how I would feel being in Mr. Haney's company.

When we pulled up in front of their nineteenth-century row house in Southwest Center City, their street was double parked with cars mostly bearing municipal tags. I swallowed hard and stepped down out of the truck.

"What's going on, G, with all the cars?" I asked.

"My parents are having a small fund-raiser and I promised them we'd stop by."

"I can't go in there. I'm not dressed for this."

"You look good, girl. Come on," he said, and grabbed me by the hand, pulling me along.

"Well, damn it, G-dog. You could've told me."

"Why, so you'd think of another fuckin' excuse?"

"G-dog, I don't think I should be meeting your parents, not tonight," I said, as we walked up the street to their house.

"Shit, you think I wanna go? Come on, it'll give my father a hard-on that I brought a date." He looked me over approvingly. "Especially you."

There were about seventy-five people throughout the house, and immediately my eyes found Mr. Haney. By the time we made our way to him, Mrs. Haney was by his side. She wasn't as matronly as she looked on television. G-dog's Caucasian mother had thinning hair, which she'd swept up into a French twist, and was dressed in a black cocktail dress. A stunning diamond necklace glittered around her neck.

"Dad, you've already met her, but, Mom, this is Tiffany Johnson. She's opening her own club in a few months. You remember, I told you."

"Nice to meet you, Tiffany. Are you from the Philadelphia area?" his mother asked, her eyes giving me the once-over while she shook my hand.

Oh boy, here goes, I thought before answering. "Yes, but my parents live in Cherry Hill now."

"And where'd you go to school, dear?"

"Mom, damn, you can't be interviewing the girl."

"It's okay. I received my bachelor's in economics from the University of Maryland," I said, all the while feeling Mr. Haney's eyes penetrating me.

"Son, sounds like she has a good head on her shoulders. You should take a hint," his father added, while smiling at me and nudging G-dog.

"Why'd you bring me here?" I whispered to G-dog when his father turned to shake the hand of the city managing director.

"Hey, he's the one with the money," he whispered back, then walked away to get us drinks, leaving me with his parents.

"Tell me, Ms. Johnson, how'd my son get chosen to go into business with a lovely lady like yourself?" Mr. Haney asked.

I could've sworn Mr. Haney's tongue circled his lips as his eyes made their way up and down my naked arms, lingering on the little bit of cleavage I was showing. Mrs. Haney was oblivious as she stood beside him nodding like a robot and smiling at others when it was appropriate. I sensed that she was totally uninterested in this party and me.

"Actually, your son contacted me when he heard I was looking for a security company," I answered, trying to ignore the throbbing sensation building up between my legs.

By now Mr. Haney's gaze had returned to mine and I felt he could see the satisfaction he'd given me.

"I see. Well, I do hope you and Greg will come by for dinner with me and my wife one night," he added, looking at his wife for approval.

Before I could answer, G-dog walked up and handed me a glass.

"Dad, I'm rolling out in a minute."

"Sure, son," he said, before turning to me and adding, "Tiffany, please do call me if you need anything."

The one person I hadn't expected to run into was Brad Lomas, Malik's friend who worked at Internal Affairs.

"Hey, Tiffany. What's going on?"

"Nothing, I'm just here with . . ."

"No need to bullshit me. I know what happened," he answered, relieving me from making a fool of myself.

"I'm not offering any excuses for my man, but that dude right there"—he nodded toward G-dog—"is bad news, so be careful."

G-dog walked up behind me, his arm around my waist.

"Hey, what's up, man?" he said to Brad, then looked at me. "You ready?"

"Yeah, sure. Goodnight, Brad."

We were quiet on the ride back down Market Street, and I didn't argue when, rather than taking me home, G-dog took me to his apartment. For the first time I put all I had into making love with him in an effort to get thoughts of his father out of my head. Afterward he sat up in bed, sweaty and satisfied, with me curled beside him.

"Tiff, I need to talk to you about something serious."

"What could be serious right now?" I asked, crossing my legs over his.

"What if I told you I could put ten grand in your pocket tax-free every week."

"G, baby, what are you talking about? Anything like that has to be illegal."

"Actually, it's not. At least not by my standards."

"Your standards? And just what is this moneymaking scheme?" I asked, sitting up and straddling him, my hands twisting his curly locks around my fingers.

"I got some people who want to do a little gambling in your basement at Teaz."

"Are you still drunk or something?"

"It's only for six months and then they'll move on to another spot."

"It's too risky. I could go to jail. Plus, who the hell are they?"

"Nobody is going to jail while my father is the damn district attorney, at least nobody he doesn't want to go."

"Even if I did consider it, I'm telling you my partners won't go for it. Definitely not Malik."

"Didn't you tell me you were the majority owner? Well, act like you got control of this thing and stop letting Malik make all your decisions. I mean, what could be wrong with a little poker and blackjack anyway? Tiffany, you're from the streets of South Philly. You know how these things work. If these boys want in, then they get in or you could have some serious problems. I mean, imagine what they could do if some of the laborers down there turned out to be nonunion guys."

I knew just what he meant: Philadelphia was a mob-controlled town. I was positive that these were the people of whom he spoke. Malik had often warned me that they might somehow try to weasel their way into Teaz, and if that happened, I was supposed to let him know immediately.

"G, I don't know."

"Awww, c'mon, girl. Do this for me, alright? Haven't I been there for you?"

"But what if Malik—"

"Fuck Malik, that nigga done moved on. Why you still sweating him? It's me and you now, and I'm going to the top, so if you wanna make moves you better come on and do this thing."

"I don't know. I mean, G, I could lose the club."

"There you go, worrying. Now, didn't my father and me come through with your permits? You know I wouldn't do anything to jeopardize your shit."

"Well, maybe. I mean, if it's only for a few months."

"Look, my security firm will make sure that nobody knows about it, so just let me handle this, okay? I promise you it'll be all good. You trust me, right?"

He'd given me no reason not to trust him. And maybe with the extra money I could eventually purchase that house in the Hamptons as Leila had suggested.

When I got home from G-dog's apartment the next morning I'd already changed my mind. I thought about calling Malik to tell him what G-dog was proposing because I knew that he detested anything illegal. But I doubted if he'd even talk to me. When I returned from taking Bruiser for his walk I was stopped by one of my neighbors, who asked me if I'd seen the morning paper. I picked up the *Philadelphia Inquirer* off the step and there on the front page I saw that one of the partners at Malik's firm had been arrested for drug possession.

I tried to reach Malik several times but was told he was out of the office. I tried his cell phone but it kept going into voice mail. I couldn't imagine what had happened. It was impossible for me to believe that Michael Covington was involved with drugs. Hell, he was fifty-two years old. Since I couldn't get through to Malik, I watched and listened to the news for most of the day, waiting to hear an update. And all I could get was that more arrests were being made.

There wasn't much else for me to do, so I cleaned the house and fixed myself some dinner. Then around 8:00 P.M., while I was sitting in the living room going through samples of velvet cording for the club, my house phone rang.

"Hello?" The caller ID read private name, private number, and I couldn't imagine who was calling.

"Tiffany, hey, it's Gregory Haney. I'm sorry to call you at home, but I have to talk to you."

"Is something wrong with Malik?" I asked, thinking maybe he'd gotten himself into trouble, too.

"Uh, kinda. But I really need to speak with you and I can't do it over the phone. Are you alone?"

"Yeah, but you shouldn't be coming by my house, should you?"

"It'll only take a minute, but I do need to see you."

The urgency in his voice coupled with the whispering made me think that maybe something was wrong, so I told him that I'd be waiting for him.

When he hadn't arrived an hour later, I began to worry even more. I was just about to pour myself a glass of wine when the doorbell rang.

"Thanks for letting me come by," he said, as he quickly strolled through the doorway.

Bruiser was putting on his vicious act, barking and trying to get around me. It was as if ever since Malik and I split, that dog had gone from mild-mannered to ferocious. I held on to his collar to keep him from attacking Mr. Haney.

"Bruiser, calm down."

"Why don't you put that mutt away so we can talk?"

"He's not a damn mutt, he's a mastiff," I answered, pushing Bruiser through the dining room and out the back door. My dog obviously didn't trust Mr. Haney.

When I returned to the living room Mr. Haney had made himself comfortable in Malik's recliner and was watching the news.

"Shame about your boyfriend's firm. Looks like they could be going down."

"I doubt that very much. I'm sure Malik will get to the bottom of it."

"If you say so, but it doesn't look good. I've seen the arrest warrant."

"What was so urgent?"

"I need you, Tiffany."

"What? Are you telling me that was all bullshit on the phone?" I asked as I walked past him.

"All I've been able to think about are those slanty eyes of yours and that silky ass skin," he said, then reached out and grabbed me by the belt of my wrap dress, sliding his hands underneath before kissing me on my bare stomach.

I pulled myself from his grip and said, "Why are you here, Mr. Haney?"

"Come on now. You know why I'm here. For the same reason you want me here. Are you going to tell me you're not lonely and worried about your boyfriend?"

"Malik is not my boyfriend. Your son is, remember?"

"So then what am I?"

"Can you please leave?" I asked him, walking toward the door to let him out.

He mocked me with his laugh and said, "That's not what you were screaming about at the club."

The mention of that night gripped me so quickly in a passion that it scared me.

"Mr. Haney, you need to get out of here right now," I said, my hand on the knob, yet still not opening the door.

"C'mon, now, lovely lady. I went to a lot of trouble to get here tonight."

"That's not my problem. Now leave," I demanded, my hands holding my dress closed.

"I'm not going away that easy and you know it."

"If you don't, I'll call . . ."

"Nobody."

I tried to think of something to say. I tried to think of who I could call to get Philadelphia's district attorney out of my house, but nobody came to mind. And as much as I didn't want to believe it, there was no denying that my pussy began to pulsate with desire for him.

He totally ignored me and I stood there, unable to move or to think of what to say to convince him that I couldn't do this again with him.

"What if you get me a drink first? Then I'll leave. Is that a deal?"

I went into the kitchen and poured a glass of wine. When I came back into the living room Mr. Haney was hanging up his suit jacket on the railing, and I noticed he was wearing a bulletproof vest, complete with a holster that held a Glock nine gun.

"Here's your drink," I said, handing him the glass. "Is all that really necessary?" I pointed at the gun.

"Of course it is. You wouldn't want me to get hurt, now, would you?"

He moved to sit beside me on the sofa, which caused me to cross my legs at the ankles and cross my arms over my chest.

"Talk to me, Tiffany. Tell me why you're always so up-tight."

"I'm not uptight—anyway, it's not that easy."

"Wait a minute. Why am I drinking alone?" he asked. Without waiting for my reply, he got up from the sofa, went into the kitchen, and came back with a glass of wine for me.

I accepted the drink and busied myself using the television remote control to channel-surf.

"That's some nice perfume you're wearing."

"Thank you," I said stiffly.

"What, you can't take my compliments either? Why don't you talk to me, Tiffany? Tell me what's on your mind. If it's Malik Skinner, maybe I can help him out."

I sipped the wine. It felt nice and warm going down, but I was determined to not let this situation get out of control.

"It's not that. It's just that this isn't right. You're G-dog's father."

"To hell with what's right. You going to tell me that you didn't feel fantastic when I made love to you, that I didn't hit all the right spots?"

There was no denying it. But I didn't want to admit it out loud, especially to him.

Leaning toward me, he traced my earlobe with the tips of his fingers and I felt myself begin to melt. I stood up to get away from him.

"Just stop it and get out, please," I begged.

"You know what confuses me? You're a beautiful and sexy woman who can have any man you want, so why are you so shocked that I want you?" he said, as if he really didn't understand.

Unwilling to answer his question, I looked away. My gaze landed on the velvet rope samples.

"What's this?" he asked, bending over to look at the samples.

Rather than answer, I went into the kitchen and poured myself another glass of wine.

"What do you say, lovely lady?" he hollered to me from the other room.

"What . . . how . . . I mean . . ." I wasn't even sure what I was answering. Suddenly Mr. Haney's hands were inside my dress. I hadn't even heard him come up behind me in the kichen. I felt so hot. I moved away from him and returned to the living room to turn up the air conditioning.

"This—this is not a good idea," I tried to say, but couldn't quite get the words out because I was drifting to that place where Mr. Haney had taken me before. I held on to the arm of the sofa and tried to make my way to the thermostat. He caught me in his arms when I began to sway back and forth.

"Here, sit down," he said, pulling me over to the recliner with him. I watched him refill my glass. He held it to my lips. "Now, come on. Drink up. I have a treat for you."

"Mr. Haney, I've had enough."

"Tiffany, be quiet now, or I'm going to have to spank your little silky ass. Now, is that what you want?"

Almost as if in slow motion, he stood up and removed his gun and holster, placing them both on the end table. I tried not to imagine what was next.

"I'm not doing this with you. You can't just come in here . . ." I tried to say more but he was already kneeling in front of me, crawling between my legs, placing kisses along my thighs.

"Here, suck on these for me so I can get you right," he mumbled, after dipping his fingers into his wineglass.

My throat was dry so I took his fingers in my mouth and

sucked off the wine. He opened my dress, dipped his fingers back in the glass, and traced my nipples. I willed my limp body to resist him but it was useless. His touch felt way too good at this point.

"Now, I'm going to make you feel good tonight, right?"

When I didn't answer right away he used the tips of his fingers to squeeze both my nipples so hard it made my eyes blink. I nodded my head.

"Good," he said, then I heard that ridiculing laugh of his. He moved one hand from my breast to press his thumb down against the soft tissue inside my vagina. I scooted closer to the edge of the chair, and he covered me with his mouth.

"Mmmm, there's nothing more intoxicating than the smell of hot pussy," he said, before pulling away and allowing me to see where my well-seasoned juices had spread themselves all over his face.

I grabbed on to the flap of his bulletproof vest, bringing him back to me. He tickled my clit with the tip of his tongue, sending riveting chills through me.

Behind him the light from the television suddenly became too bright so I closed my eyes. I could hear Mr. Haney's voice, so close, almost as if he were in the room with me, but I knew he was on the television. No . . . he was here with me. I must be confused. Was it Mr. Haney my lover talking to me or the district attorney? The television was replaying one of his interviews. Both of their voices merged.

"You know I'm going to make this pussy sore tonight," he said, torturing me by dipping his fingers from my pussy to my asshole.

My mouth was numb but my eyes begged him to make love to me. I closed my eyes for a moment and when I opened them again, he'd put the chair in the reclining position, and spread my legs over each side.

"Open that pussy for me, Tiffany. I don't have a lot of time," he said, his voice stern and commanding.

I relented and did as he asked, using my hands to separate and ready myself for his entry. But he took his time, dropping his pants and letting his large dick fall out. He stroked himself, long and hard, then walked over to me and rubbed his dick back and forth across my face. When finally I couldn't take any more of his teasing, I wrapped my hands around his dick and brought him into my mouth, relishing its taste. But he wasn't able to take that for long, so he withdrew from my mouth, then forcibly shoved his dick in, then out, of my pussy until my juices were dripping onto the chair.

"Ouuuuchhhhhh," I screamed in pain as much as in pleasure as the head of Mr. Haney's dick reached the basement of my pussy.

Holding on to my knees, he dipped in and out and then whirled his dick around, plunging it farther and farther into the cavity of my body. Sounds I'd never heard before escaped my mouth.

"Don't cry, you nasty bitch. You know you can take it."

No man had ever talked to me like that. Had ever called me a bitch while making love. But that wasn't what we were doing.

A sheepish grin came across his face and I thought I could

even hear him tell me how much he loved my dark fudge while he kissed me, passionately, like a man who was in love. I could barely breathe as he talked into my mouth.

"Nobody, you hear me, nobody has ever been able to take this dick like you do. I love you, Tiffany."

He must've realized that he was saying things that made him sound weak and vulnerable because he pulled away, leaving my mouth open and hungry for him. I stared up at him, my expression full of questions. I tried to speak but couldn't open my mouth. I thought he was going to quench my thirst but he let the wine run over my lips, down my breasts and between my legs. And his mouth was there to take it all in.

But I knew that Mr. Haney was far from finished. The last thing I allowed myself to remember before drifting off into pure ecstasy was the feel of the velvet ropes as Mr. Haney tied my wrists to the legs of the couch.

7

ANOTHER CHANCE

From somewhere in my unconsciousness I was abruptly awakened by Bruiser's loud barking, but I had no idea where it was coming from. Finding myself cramped in a tight ball in Malik's recliner, I surveyed the room from swollen eyes. When I put my feet down on the floor pain shot through me and I noticed that from my breasts down, I was covered with dried lavender candle wax. My God, what had Mr. Haney done to me? There were no bruises though my thighs were sore, as were my legs and arms, as if I'd been beaten. I wanted to shout out to Bruiser to shut up, but my lips were cracked and dry and my gums were sore.

I was so disoriented that I had no idea what time or day it

was. I picked up the remote from the floor to turn off the loud sounds of the morning news. But I stopped when I saw Mr. Haney's face and heard his voice detailing the arrests he'd made overnight. Was it possible I was hallucinating?

Before I could get to Bruiser, I went to the refrigerator, where there was only one bottle of spring water left. I drank that and then turned on the faucet and filled my hands with water repeatedly, trying to quench my thirst. I unlocked the back door to let in Bruiser, who trampled me to the floor. I lay there looking up at him while he licked at my face. Crawling, I made my way from the kitchen to the stairs, holding on to the railing as a guide to get to my room. I climbed into bed.

It had to have been hours later when I woke up, sweaty and dehydrated. I could see the streetlights shining through my curtains. I couldn't hear any noise outside above the banging in my head. Try as I might, I couldn't put together the pieces of Mr. Haney's visit, and judging from my inability to recall all the details, I was sure he'd put something in my drink, probably Ecstasy. I thought about the irony of him giving me Ecstasy while as DA he was running a drug sting operation. Thinking expended way more energy than I had so I stopped. Instead I used what energy I had left to take a shower and scrape candle wax from my body. Afterward, I was too drained to do anything else but climb back under my covers.

Just as I was drifting back to sleep, I heard the phone ringing in the distance. It sounded like two phones, two different rings. I groped around in the darkened room for the cell phone and before I could say hello I heard my nephew's crying voice.

"Auntie Tiff, Auntie Tiff," my nephew Kareem screamed to me, "something's wrong with Mommy."

"Huh, Kareem, what are you talking about?" I asked, sitting up in bed, my voice hoarse.

He kept crying and didn't answer me.

"Kareem, where's your mother at?"

"She's right there in the corner but she's . . . Auntie Tiff, I'm scared."

Stumbling out of bed, I searched around the bedroom for my cordless phone.

"Stop crying, honey, and tell Auntie what's wrong. Give the phone to your mommy."

"I'm scared . . . I don't wanna go over there."

I could hear Raphael and Anthony in the background crying. I looked over at the clock. It was 1:00 A.M.

While keeping Kareem on the cell phone, I dialed 911 from the house phone and told the operator I wasn't sure what the situation was after giving him Kamille's address.

"Auntie is going to keep talking to you until I get there, okay?" I said, going to the armoire and quickly pulling on a pair of jeans and a T-shirt.

"I'm scared, Auntie Tiff. Hurry up."

"It's okay, Kareem. Auntie is on her way. You stay right there, okay?"

I arrived at Kamille's house just as the ambulance was pulling up. There we found three frightened children and my unconscious sister.

While the paramedics worked at reviving her, I took the boys downstairs and called my parents. I also phoned Essence, G-dog, and, for some reason, Malik.

After getting a neighbor to watch the boys, I drove to St. Agnes Hospital. Essence was already there, along with a man who'd probably been her date for the night. Shortly afterward my parents arrived.

While we waited for the doctors to tell us something I paced the floor, thinking of all the things I would say to my sister. I didn't care whose fault it was, I was going to apologize for all the hurtful things I'd said to her. But I couldn't keep my thoughts straight. I'd already drunk two cans of soda and a half cup of coffee, which only added to my nervousness. I was so confused. Where the hell was G-dog? Why was he always out of town, especially now when I needed him? And what about last night when I needed him to keep his father away from me? My nerves were frazzled and every hole on my body was sore from having been with Mr. Haney. My piercing headache made me sit down on the vinyl bench in the waiting room. Drained, I lowered my head and began to cry. Essence heard me whimpering, came over, and put her arm around my shoulders.

"She's going to be alright," she said, trying to soothe me. Then her tone changed when she said, "What's *he* doing here with *her?*"

I wasn't sure who she was talking about. I looked in the direction of her gaze and saw Malik coming through the revolving doors dressed in a black tuxedo. Beside him was a white woman from his office.

He introduced his date to everyone, and I managed to say hello and have respect for my family by not lashing out at him about bringing his woman along. However, she must've noticed the tension because she told him she'd wait in the car. My parents went off to the cafeteria to get something to drink.

"What happened, Tiff?"

"We don't know, but they think she took something."

"Aww, shit. Thanks for calling me," he said, stroking his mustache.

"Well, under the circumstances I thought you might want to know," I said, turning my head from him.

"There are no circumstances. I used to be part of this family until you lost your mind," he said, his voice stern.

I jumped up, my hands at his chest, pushing him backward. "I assume you still are, Malik! It's not like I don't know you're still fucking my sister."

With his eyes wide with surprise, he held on to my wrists.

"Tiffany, you're going crazy. Are you drunk again?"

Essence moved to stand between us. "Listen, you two. This isn't the time for your bullshit. Something is seriously wrong with Kamille and you better be damn focused on that."

"You're right, I'm sorry," Malik said. "But I have to admit that I thought it might come to this."

"Come to what? Do you know what's wrong with my sister? What did you do to her, Malik? Is she pregnant with another one of your babies?" I yelled.

"Tiffany, stop this shit. You're making a fool of yourself. What the hell is wrong with you?"

"Tell me what's going on, Malik," I shouted into his face.

My parents returned from the cafeteria and we stood in a semicircle around Malik, waiting for his response.

"Your sister called me a few weeks ago when the test results came back and . . ." He paused and looked at my parents before continuing.

"And what?" I prompted.

"The results were negative, Tiffany. But that wasn't the only reason she was calling. She's kinda gotten herself hooked on that Ecstasy."

I had mixed feelings—relief that Malik wasn't Kareem's father and anger that my sister had been using drugs. Why had she called him?

"That's bullshit. Kamille doesn't mess with drugs," I said, defending my sister as I knew her.

"Tiffany, he's right. This isn't the first time she's taken it," Essence said from beside me.

"Damn it, why didn't you tell me, Essence?"

"Like you would have heard me. Remember, you weren't listening to what anybody had to say."

My mother jumped in, too. "You should've been taking care of your sister. Then maybe none of this would have happened."

"Doesn't anybody care about how I was feeling, what I was going through?"

My father's angry voice spoke over everyone. "Damn it, everybody shut the hell up. Now, here comes the doctor. Malik and Essence, tell him what you know."

The doctor had suspected Kamille had taken drugs, but now Malik was able to confirm that it was Ecstasy. The doctor didn't think she'd intentionally overdosed, but there was a buildup of it in her bloodstream. Though she appeared to be out of danger, the doctor couldn't be positive until she regained consciousness.

Kamille woke up three hours later. I waited until everyone left her room before going inside. I wasn't looking forward to facing her; somehow I felt like this was entirely my fault. Why couldn't I just have been patient?

When I walked in her room she'd dozed off again. Her face was pale and she looked weak and helpless with the oxygen tube in her nose and an IV in her arm. After a few minutes her eyes flitted open and I sat beside her on the bed. We both started talking and crying simultaneously.

"Sis, I'm so sorry," she cried to me.

"No, it's okay. I'm sorry. I acted like an ass."

"Tiffany, you have to take Malik back. He loves you. Kareem's not his."

"Yes, honey, I know. But why didn't you say something when you first found out or when I came to your house that night?"

"I don't know. I guess I didn't think it mattered anymore. I just figured you hated me and that would never change. I mean, sis, I did the worst thing imaginable. I let a man come between us. Then I was so spaced out on that shit I couldn't think straight."

"No, I came between us when I didn't listen to you or Malik."

"What are you going to do about him? He loves you." Kamille began to cry again. "I swear I didn't mean to hurt

you. It was so long ago I just wanted to forget about it." I
wiped her tears with my hands, paying no attention to the
ones that fell from my own eyes.

I sat up on the side of the bed massaging her hands. "Let's
not worry about me and Malik right now. I want to know
who gave you this Ecstasy and why you've been taking it.
Kamille, you've never done drugs."

"It's in every club across the city. You can get it anywhere."

I had done Ecstasy myself and I knew all too well it was a
dangerous substance. "Well, I promise you this. I'm going to
find out who's pushing this shit in the city and I'm gonna
make sure he goes to jail. But why'd you take it, sweetie?"

She turned her head from me and I used my hands to
turn it back around.

"I don't know. I tried it like twice, and then when everything happened . . . I don't know, I just couldn't stop taking
it. It just melted everything away. Like I wasn't really a bad
person."

"Don't say that. You're not a bad person. I'm the one who
wouldn't listen. But you know I love you, Kamille. Please
promise me you won't take that shit again." And I made a
silent promise to myself at that moment that I would never
take it again, either.

"I won't," Kamille softly promised. Then she added,
"Tiffany, I knew it was wrong to use E, but it felt so good."

I remained silent to encourage my sister to tell me why
she felt she had to use drugs. I didn't think it was the time to
tell her about my experience with Ecstasy.

"It, it makes you so sensitive, like every touch is multiplied. I swear it makes everything—every worry, every inhibition—melt away. On that stuff you'd probably sleep with anybody, you're so horny. The only drawback is that after it wears off you feel really thirsty and as if someone's beat every part of your body."

Kamille's description of the effects of Ecstasy sounded so similar to how I felt just that morning. I was sure Mr. Haney had used it to drug me into having sex with him the night before.

"Isn't it expensive?" I asked, wondering how much Mr. Haney spent on his underhanded seduction.

"About thirty dollars a tablet, or it can come in a liquid. I guess you don't know anything about it, huh?"

"I'm starting to know about it. So, I guess you turned to E and I turned to drinking."

"You, a drunk?"

"Girl, your sister was about ready to join Alcoholics Anonymous."

We both laughed, but neither of us thought it was really funny.

"What's wrong, sis?" she asked.

"Huh, oh, nothing. I just remember feeling that way," I said, as thoughts of Mr. Haney feeding me the little white pill replayed in my head.

"You took E?" she asked, her eyes wide in shock.

"We can talk about that later. Right now why don't we just concentrate on you getting better?"

We sat in silence for a moment, happy to be in each other's company again after such a long time.

"Sis, there's something else, too, something good," she said, a smile spreading across her cracked lips.

"What is it, baby? What is it?" I asked, tucking the covers around her.

"My parents, I mean my birth father, I think I'm getting closer to finding out who he is."

"That's so good, Kamille. What about your birth mother?"

Tears rolled from her eyes, and I could only imagine the worst, that she'd gone to this woman and been rejected. "Did she hurt you, Kamille? What'd she say?"

"No, it's not that. She's dead. She died about two years ago."

"I'm so sorry. That must've been horrible for you to find out after all this time. I can't believe I wasn't there for you."

"It's okay. The investigator says he's going to call me when he gets the details about my father, but he suspects he's here, in Philly. Can you go with me when it's time to meet him?"

"Of course, Kamille, whatever you want. God, I'm so sorry I haven't been there for you," I said, choking back tears, trying to be strong for her.

"Thanks, sis . . ." Kamille began to drift off. "I love you, sis. Don't leave me here by myself, okay?"

"I love you, too," I said, then climbed into bed beside her and stayed there until the next morning, when she was released.

8

BLIND BET

It was time for me to apologize to Malik for my behavior at the hospital. A week after Kamille's overdose I realized that I had been selfish to think that I had been the only one affected by her and Malik's brief encounter. Finally gathering up the nerve, I phoned him at work. I was curious to see if there was any way to salvage our relationship. Kamille had become insistent that I not only get Malik back but that I continue with my plans to marry him even though we were both in relationships with other people.

"Hey, Malik. It's me, Tiffany."

"I know who it is. The question is, what do you want?"

"Look, I'm sorry about what happened at the hospital. Actually, I'm sorry about a lot of things. What I was calling for was to see if you'd have lunch with me."

"That's it. Lunch? Sure, Tiffany, but damn, I thought you were calling to cuss me out again."

"Not hardly. All that's in the past, believe me. I would just like to talk with you."

"Sure. How's tomorrow afternoon?"

"That's perfect."

Kamille took a vacation day from work so she could decide what I should wear. "Something sexy, something short, something easy to remove," she'd suggested. And when I answered the door for her that morning she was bringing not only coffee and scones but a silk crepe de chine, tangerine-colored dress with mother-of-pearl clasps at the shoulders.

I was growing nervous that Malik would cancel when he called to tell me he was running late and asked if we could make our lunch date a dinner instead. I had no choice but to agree and was actually hoping that meant he wanted to spend more time with me. I made reservations for us at the blues club Warmdaddy's on Front Street. I was running a few minutes late from trying to find a parking space, and when I got to the dining room Malik was caught off guard by my sexy and revealing dress.

He jumped up from his seat and strode across the room to greet me. "You look so good, Tiffany. I don't think I've ever seen you like this."

"Really? You don't think it's too revealing?"

"Hell yes. Hey, come on now. You can't blame a brother for not wanting anybody else to see his goods," he joked, while holding my hand and leading me to our table.

He pulled out my chair but not before kissing me on the

cheek. "Here, sit down," he said, then leaned over and took a whiff of my neck. "And you smell good, too. Is that something new?"

"You've always been good at guessing."

"No more guesses for me."

We ordered drinks and I kept mine light by simply ordering a Mocktini, cranberry and seltzer, while Malik chose a Rémy Martin. While waiting for the band to play we talked about everything except the obvious. I'm sure neither of us was in a hurry to get to it. To continue our small talk, I asked him about his partner, Michael Covington, who'd been arrested a few days earlier.

"Tiffany, you have no idea how ridiculous this all is. Mike would never be involved with drugs. You remember a few years back when his nephew died from an overdose? Well, since then he barely even drinks. Somebody was plain out to get him, or us, meaning the firm."

"Why do you think he was set up?"

"I don't know yet. But I bet my career that Greg Haney's office has something to do with all this."

My stomach flipped at the mention of the DA's name, and I nibbled on my olive, hoping that Malik didn't notice any change in my facial expression.

"Why would they do that?"

"Well, that's easy enough to answer." He leaned in closer so the other diners couldn't hear. "Michael was thinking about running for mayor and mentioned it to a few of his political friends. Within a week his car is pulled over for no reason and he's found with an eighth of an ounce of cocaine.

And to top that shit off we're holding the witness who can send five of Haney's top cops up the river for being on the take from some drug dealers."

"Malik, I didn't realize how bad the drug thing was in the city. Five cops? That isn't good at all. Is Michael going to be able to get off? Do you think this onslaught of drugs will make its way to Teaz? I'm sorry, I'm asking too many questions."

"No, it's perfectly alright. I'm glad to see you're interested in what's going on. And that's the other reason I wanted to talk to you. I want you to be very careful when the club opens. There's no doubt your place will be a target for every hustler of every drug in town."

"You're scaring me, Malik," I said, but what was really scaring me was that I had this unnerving feeling that the Haneys were somehow involved.

"But hey, woman, I don't want to spend all my time talking about business and worrying you."

"It's okay, I don't mind at all. Actually, I miss talking to you about your work."

"That's good to hear, because from the looks of the summer I thought you'd never talk to me."

"It's not that, it was just that I was in shock when I heard you two in the kitchen that night."

"And you had every right to be. But I, too, have some things to say."

"What's that?" I asked.

He waited until the waitress set down our food before he answered. "Tiffany, I need you to understand where I'm at on some things. You see, I'm still hoping we can . . ." He paused when his cell phone went off, then spoke into it. "Hey, man. What's up?"

I had no idea who was on the other end.

"Michael, don't fuck around with me like that. I been working on this thing too hard."

It didn't sound good.

"Alright, I'm on my way," he said, looking at me for approval.

I nodded to let him know I understood. He hung up the phone and placed his hand over mine in consolation.

"Tiffany, I'm so sorry, but I have to go and handle this."

"What's wrong, Malik? What happened?"

He looked at me long and hard, as if trying to decide if he should tell me.

"The district attorney wants to meet with me to talk about the case against his cops. But, Tiffany, this is very confidential, so please don't say anything to anyone, okay? Especially his son."

"Malik, you can trust me."

"I know I can. I also want you to know that I'm not finished having this conversation with you. Listen, I'm going to call you because I want to stop by and get a tour of the club before opening night."

"I'd like that."

The next morning, before meeting up with Kamille for a debriefing on my short date with Malik, I left the house and went to a much needed appointment with my hair stylist. If

Malik thought I was beautiful last night, then I really had a surprise for him next time.

When I explained to Shay what I wanted her to do with my hair, she was reluctant to do something so drastic, but after a little begging and promises to give her free passes to Teaz, she finally got out the scissors. Three hours later I'd been transformed. When she was finished even I was scared to look in the mirror. But the results were stunning and just like I'd imagined. My jet black, straight hair was now short and spiky with muted blond highlights. There was barely enough to comb. My new look erased all traces of the old me.

Afterward I met up with a very surprised Kamille.

"What the hell did you do?"

"Please tell me you like it. I'll die if you don't."

"I love it! It's just that I'm in shock. You just look so damn different."

"I feel different, too. I feel naked," I said, rubbing my hands through my hair.

We'd made plans to go shopping so we headed out to the mall. During our ride out Route 76 to King of Prussia we talked endlessly about an interview my sister had had with an accounting firm and what she planned to do with the ten-thousand-dollar increase in salary she'd get with the job. I hadn't seen my sister so excited about anything in a long time. I could only imagine how bad I'd have felt if I hadn't been able to share this moment with her.

When I recounted to her my brief date with Malik, she wasn't daunted, holding on to the hope that there was still a chance for us. I also told her that Dad had phoned and wanted us to come for dinner, that is, whenever I could get away from the club.

Once we were at the mall, my sister took over. Shopping for clothes had never been my thing, I just did it when I needed something for an event. Kamille usually picked up things for me. During this shopping spree I could see that my style was about to change. Buying clothes for one night wasn't enough. We needed, especially me, an entirely new wardrobe. If I'd gone on a shopping spree like that with Malik, he would've killed me. But I knew big things were about to happen in my life. How could they not when I looked good, smelled good, and was about to open the hottest club in the country? After visiting damn near every department store and boutique in the plaza, I was exhausted. Kamille was still raring to go. We had to make a trip to the car just to stash our bags before getting some lunch.

While we sat in the food court gobbling up pizza I decided it would be a good time to tell Kamille about the poker and blackjack games that G-dog was proposing to host in the basement of the club. However, I still wasn't ready to tell her about what had happened with his father and was actually hoping there'd be no need to do so.

"Bad idea, sis. Real bad idea. How'd you let yourself get pushed into a corner with G-dog? I mean, first he's providing the security and now this. When did you become so hypnotized by money?"

"I don't know. I guess I just realized how powerful it is. What should I do about G-dog wanting to put a casino in the basement?"

"For starters, you could tell Malik. Better yet, tell that dog's father, the big-time DA."

A dark shadow must've covered my face. Kamille immediately picked up on it and asked, "Is there something you're not telling me?"

I started to lie, but she reminded me that we weren't holding back any secrets from each other.

"I know we said no secrets, but I'm just not ready to discuss it yet. Is that okay?"

She slurped up the last of her soda, her eyes steady on me. "When will you be ready?"

"Let's get the club open first, okay?"

Kamille didn't look pleased but she nodded.

"I have made one decision I think you'll be happy about."

"What! What is it?"

"I think I do want to try to get Malik back."

"You *think?* Sis, are you crazy? You better get him back from them stuck-up bitches he's been seeing. But wait a minute. Where will that leave dog boy and the club?"

I cracked up at her reference to G-dog, and said, "I haven't quite figured that out yet."

The next afternoon around 4:30 G-dog and I met Leila at the club. I'd already spoken to her about overseeing the basement operations and she seemed fine with the idea. They'd already sent over private contractors to survey the space in the basement and in just a few days they'd transformed it into a small casino. There was a private entrance inside the club and another from outside in the alleyway. They'd set up poker, blackjack, and craps tables, a small bar, and a few booths for those who weren't playing. In order to fit all the casino stuff in the basement, I had to find new storage space for Teaz's supplies. Luckily, next door to Teaz was an empty building that G-dog's father owned that I could use for storage. I wasn't too happy about that and hadn't actually thought through what to do about storage, but it was a quick fix so I didn't complain.

The casino's hours of operation were the same as Teaz's so the gambling activity would go unnoticed. As Leila and G-dog discussed the details, I found it interesting that they understood so well what had to be done. Leila seemed quite experienced at working an operation of this nature. She'd been in the business longer than I had, so I'm sure she'd been through this routine before at other clubs.

After they'd both left and I'd locked up the club, I was surprised to see Malik come strolling from around the corner of Sansom Street.

"Hey, look at you! You look so hot!"

I was so glad to see him and receive his compliment that I blushed.

"Come on, turn around and let me see it all," he eagerly said, spinning me around. "Damn, it took the summer from hell to bring all this out."

"Alright, Malik. You're embarrassing me now," I said, as the after-work rush hour crowd slowed down on Market Street to see what all the commotion was about.

"I hope I'm not interrupting anything," Malik said.

"Of course not. I'm just surprised to see you, that's all."

"Well, I was hoping to get the grand tour before the fireworks begin. You have a minute?"

"It's fine. I mean, I have dinner with my parents tonight but I have a few minutes. Come on," I said as he followed me inside.

"I love your hair, this whole new look," he said, placing his hands on my waist.

"Thanks. Thank you, Malik," I stammered, totally caught off guard by the affection he displayed. He couldn't seem to stop touching me and I was enjoying every moment.

"Turn around and let me see," he said, this time referring to the tight low-riding jeans and T-shirt I wore.

Leaning over, he whispered his good news into my ear. "I made partner today."

I think I smiled harder than he did and my natural reaction was to hug him.

"Oh, Malik, that's wonderful. Congratulations!" I exclaimed, flinging my arms around his neck.

"I finally did it, huh? I want you to know, I came here to celebrate with you. But first I wanna see the club."

"Okay, here goes," I said, then adjusted the lights inside the electrical closet to show how the club would look when it was open. It even took me aback when I looked at everything and began to go over the layout of the club with Malik. Now that it was complete, Teaz spanned twenty-five hundred square feet of space and could hold a crowd of eight hundred. There were two mirrored ramps that led into the club and at the end of the hall was a large VIP space. From this area people, namely celebrities or those who could afford to rent the room, could feel comfortable making things happen without the distraction and intrusion of onlookers. Across from the VIP section were high-top cocktail tables and stools—all of which looked out on the newly laid hardwood dance floor that had a warm glow from the lights that reflected off the square frosted glass in the middle. It made it seem as if you'd be dancing on air. There were two bars, one on either side of the hall, both made of slate, and they separated the dance floor from people who wanted to sit and chat. Everything was black and sleek, with touches of crimson red and deep violet. Custom-made chairs and banquettes gave the area a secluded loungy feel.

Malik followed me up the stairs to the upper level, where there were two additional VIP rooms that had twenty-five-inch LCD screens on which to watch the action happening in the club, and each VIP room contained its own bar and bathroom. Though I'd had a part in designing Teaz, the beauty of the club still dazzled me, especially its new smell and all of the glistening top-shelf bottles that lined the shelves behind the bars.

Malik wasn't saying much as I explained the place to him. I was surprised that after taking two calls on his cell phone, he shut it off and put it in his pocket. When we entered the sound studio with its state-of-the-art equipment, I tried to remember the directions Essence had given us if we needed to play music without a DJ. It worked.

The music came on and was loud as hell, but Fat Joe's beat made my body instantly begin to dip and "Lean Back."

"What do you think?" I asked, as I felt Malik's swaying body moving against mine.

"I think this place is going to blow the lid off Philly. It's spectacular!"

"That's what I'm hoping."

As I moved to the music I looked out over the main floor of Teaz, or my little empire, as my sister referred to it. Chandeliers hung over the dance floor and billowy drapes that matched the club's contemporary furnishings covered the walls from floor to ceiling. A light fog filled the room.

Even I, who had approved everything, was dazzled by the glitzy and decadent beauty of Teaz. I'd always hoped Teaz would have the sparkle that harkened back to the days of Studio 54, with people clamoring outside just to get five minutes on the dance floor, knowing that, no matter who they came as, they'd feel like a star the second they stepped inside the door.

Malik stood behind me and said, "Woman, do you know how proud I am of you?"

"You're part of this, too."

"But this was your dream. Come on," he said, taking me in his arms to sway with him. And I was glad to do so. The beat of the music changed from rap to Alicia Keys's "If I Ain't Got You." I slowed the motion of my body as Malik wrapped his arms around me. Malik sang with her, ". . . it don't mean nothing if I ain't got you. . . ."

I found myself getting filled up with emotion. "Malik, listen, I'm sorry about the way I reacted."

He held one hand at the small of my back, and the other he used to play in my short hair.

"Hey, shhhh. Not now. And for real, Tiffany, you had every right to react the way you did. Now, I have some things to say to you. I made a big mistake by not telling you. It was only because I was so afraid that things would turn out the way they did. You weren't supposed to understand and I was wrong to think that you should. But I swear, baby, it was all because I didn't want to lose you. I was less than a man by not telling you as soon as I figured out who Kamille was, but I now realize that mistake almost cost me you."

"Almost?" I whispered.

"That's right, because I love you and I don't doubt that you feel the same way."

"But, Malik, we've gone in two different directions. What about—" Rather than let me finish, his lips lightly brushed against mine. All I could do was part them for him. As if being awakened from a dream, I heard someone shouting up from the main floor of the club, "Tiff, are you in here?" It was my sister.

"Umm, yeah, we're up here. I mean, I'm up here," I said, while Malik laughed at my stammering.

Looking up into the booth, she saw who I was with. "Awww, damn, I really didn't want to interrupt you two, but I saw your truck outside and we're supposed to go to dinner at Mommy's."

Malik came down the steps behind me, his hands around my waist. "No, it's okay. I was just showing Malik the club."

"Mmmm, looks like more than that to me. What's up, Malik?"

"Hey, Kamille. Listen, I'll let you two get going. We'll continue this later, okay, woman?" he said, then kissed me on the cheek and walked across the dance floor and out the door.

Shaking me by the shoulders, Kamille screamed, "Tiff, Tiff, I'm so happy you two are getting back together. This is great!"

"Calm down, we just kinda got caught up in the music. I don't think anything is really going to happen. Plus, every time we get to talking something comes up."

"Tiff, take it from me, you love that man and he loves you, too. It's only a matter of time."

"Girl, stop it. You want to ride with me or what?"

"Sure, but first I want you to sit down, 'cause I have to talk to you."

"What is it?" I asked, as I walked through the club still in a daze from the things Malik had said.

"It's about the investigator. He's got a good lead and I'm scared as hell."

"On your father? Hey, it's no time to be scared now. I told you I'd be with you every step of the way. Now, what did he say?"

"He is here, Tiffany. Right here in Philly!"

"Kamille, you must be ecstatic. When are we gonna find out who he is?"

"The investigator said in a few weeks maybe. I'm so excited. I mean, what will I say to him? How should I introduce myself? Do I just walk right up to him and tell him I'm the daughter he gave away? What if he has a wife and family, or what if he doesn't even care?"

"Stop all that right now. You're going to drive yourself crazy before you even meet him. Let's just wait until we get the details, then we'll figure out what the next step is, alright?"

"Whatever you say, sis, but I'm telling you, regardless of what happens, I want to see this man face-to-face."

"And you will, Kamille. I promise you. C'mon, let's go. We're going to be late."

We made our way over the Ben Franklin Bridge to our parents' house. I hadn't been back since that awful Memorial Day and I was a little anxious. I knew I needed to mend whatever hard feelings still were hanging around. It was blazing hot with a threat of rain on this humid September night, but I felt good. We'd stopped and brought my mother some roses and my dad some cigars to take the edge off, because I knew my father would have some choice words for the both of us.

My parents weren't in the kitchen when we arrived, but from the smell of fried fish I knew we'd find them on the back deck using my father's deep fryer. Walking through the house, I stopped to look at the pictures hanging on the wall in the family room. Without fail, every two years we took a family portrait and hung it with the others we'd been taking since childhood. We were about due for a new one.

"Hey, Mom, Dad," we both said almost simultaneously as we stepped onto the deck.

"Now, here's my girls," my mother responded, getting up from the table.

"'Bout time you got here. I'm starving," my dad added. "C'mon, Rose, let's get the food on the table."

My mother scurried about, bringing salad from the refrigerator and baked beans from the oven while Dad removed the last few pieces of fish from the fryer.

The conversation during dinner was light and mostly

consisted of talk about my sister's possible new job and my brother's baseball career. Eventually it came around to me and Kamille.

Dad pushed his chair back from the table. "Listen, I know you girls went through a tough time at the beginning of the summer, but I can't believe—"

Not willing to be reprimanded, Kamille cut him off. "Dad, it's over. We're fine now."

"Be quiet. I'm doing the talking. Like I was saying, it shouldn't have taken your brush with death to bring you two back together."

"You're right. I'm sorry, Dad," I said.

"Now, Tiffany, you know I love Malik like a son and probably always will, but no Negro is coming between my daughters. First off, Kamille, I told you this months ago, you should've informed your sister as soon as you knew who Malik was."

"I wanted to. I just didn't know how."

"And, Tiffany, don't you ever, I don't care what the circumstances are, disown this family. Am I clear?"

"Yes, sir."

"Sammy, please, can we just get on with dessert?"

"Alright, okay. I'm just glad you two got your shit together."

Lying in bed that night, I thought through all that had happened over the last few months. If Kamille hadn't almost died from the Ecstasy she'd been taking, would I have ever come to my senses? I was positive that Teaz wouldn't be opening in just a few short days if Kamille and I hadn't got back together. I just would've continued to drown myself in alcohol. Somehow our weaknesses had brought us back together, forming a stronger bond than before, and I knew that no matter what, I would never give up on my sister again.

I also thought about the Haney men and the time I'd spent with each of them. Mr. Haney had given me Ecstasy once, and slipped it in my drink another time. And he was the DA, had been on TV talking about cracking down on the drug trade in this city. I wasn't sure what to do about it, and was hoping that all of that was in the past now that I was stronger.

I was certain, though, that if Malik and I had any chance at reconciliation I had to put my thoughts about Mr. Haney behind me. And as for G-dog, well, once Malik and I finished our conversation, I'd tell him it was over. And if there was a problem with his contract with the club, I'd let Malik handle that, too. So, unbeknownst to Malik, everything now rested on him.

9

LABOR DAY

All week people were in and out of my office, each with his or her own set of problems. Leila stopped in frequently, keeping me updated on the fluctuating prices of alcohol, which was our highest expense.

I met with Jeff to review the final details of what needed to be finished before opening night. I was already wearing two cell phones, one for the club and one for my personal use. At the end of each day I met with the club's publicist and Kamille to go over the minute-by-minute agenda for opening night.

And as if the pace wasn't frantic enough, Essence was returning from Rhode Island after having been there for two days attending the funeral of one of her aunts. I had to not only update her on the last-minute activities but also tell her about the crap games in the basement.

"Are you outta your fucking mind? Why would you agree to some shit like that?"

"Same thing I said," I heard Kamille echo from behind me.

"It's only for a few months and we won't have to touch anything. I've already agreed to let Leila handle it."

"How'd she weasel her way into this?" Essence asked.

I waited for Leila to say something, but she just kept working silently behind the bar, stocking the shelves.

"Can you keep your voice down?" I hissed.

"I don't like her and you know that."

"C'mon, Essence, you have absolutely nothing to back up that statement."

"She just seems sneaky. I mean, first she shows up here and now y'all all chummy and she's part of this whole G-dog plan."

"Well, honestly, we don't have a choice. It's people bigger than us who want to have it here."

"Don't give me that mob shit. Ain't no kingpins around here, especially since Merlino got sent up. Hell, G-dog is the only one who thinks he's a damn king, and as far as I'm concerned he ain't shit."

"It doesn't matter who the kingpin is and a few months isn't going to hurt us. I don't want this place burned down."

"Yeah, and what if Malik finds out?"

"I'll deal with that," I said, realizing I had to make sure Malik never found out about the casino. Malik absolutely detested anything illegal.

That night I'd set my alarm for 7:00 A.M., but at 7:45 I was still lying in bed, having had barely three hours' sleep. Opening night at Club Teaz was only hours away. I turned on the television and the first thing I saw was Mr. and Mrs. Haney hosting a Labor Day barbeque for the homeless at a shelter in Kensington. I switched off the television and turned on the clock radio, listening to the stations we'd paid to feature spots announcing our opening.

I took my time with my morning rituals. I had a cup of coffee and a bagel, and took Bruiser for a walk, hoping the fresh air might shock my senses. Then I went back inside, got dressed, and headed off to the club, where I would do the walk-through with my management team to put out any last-minute fires.

By 9:00 A.M. the entire staff was present. Even my sister was on time. It was hard to believe we'd actually gotten this far. I gave a speech of sorts, stating my expectations for Teaz employees. I was sure to emphasize that I wanted everyone to have a good time, employees and guests alike. I'd been to too many clubs where the staff hated their jobs because they were worked into the ground. Teaz would be different. The staff received cash bonuses to encourage working hard and taking their service up a notch.

After taking the final tour of the space I made my way to what would be my home away from home, my office. It had a large desk, a slim modern cotton-velvet couch, and four monitors on which I could view the cash registers at the bar, the club, the basement, and the exit doors. For most of the day I answered questions, took phone calls, and handled PR.

My anxieties were so high at that point that I probably got more in the way than anything else by trying to make sure everything was perfect. Finally, Essence and Kamille insisted I go home and relax.

I left the club around three o'clock to get dressed for a seven o'clock VIP reception. This reception was by invitation only and was mainly for the media, other club owners, beverage company executives, record label promoters, and special interest parties. For the grand opening I chose a sexy black tuxedo jacket and matching pants that had to be tailored to fit my small waist. Maybe now I could be like Leila and look a little boyish, too.

When I returned to the club, via limo courtesy of G-dog, the red carpet was being rolled out and the chasing lights outside the club were being set up alongside television crews taking their posts on the curbs. This was when I began to get nervous, but it was too late to second-guess myself now.

I entered the club through a side door, and surveyed the scene inside and outside the club from the monitors in my office. Twenty minutes later, when I entered the main room, the buzz of conversation drowned out the music as people explored the club, trying to soak the place in. I took my time walking around to greet my guests and take interviews and photographs. I could see editors and publishers from our local papers as well as reporters from magazines from *FEDS* to *Vanity Fair* and I could hear BET gearing up for a live feed:

"Tonight is the opening night of the exquisite Teaz nightclub in Philadelphia. It's designed for the rich and famous and the night promises to be one filled with glamour and excitement."

When I finished the BET interview Kamille pulled me away to introduce me to a producer from MTV's *Real World*. He was there to film the opening of the club and talk to me about doing a reality series based on the nightclub industry with Teaz as its focus.

The media, guests, and celebrities were pulling me in so many directions I was soon dizzy from all the excitement and loving every minute of it. Young Huli and his entourage had also arrived, claiming their VIP space for the night. I was so proud of my brother and I reflected that I had Malik to thank for that, since he was handling his affairs.

Things were starting off well, but I was curious as to why two people hadn't arrived yet—Malik and G-dog. But no sooner than I thought this, I saw Malik wearing a bright smile and wandering around the club doing his own meet and greet. However, posted on his arm was Alex, the same anorexic woman who'd been with him at the hospital. A wave of jealousy swept over me, but I swallowed all that and walked up to greet them.

"Thanks for inviting us, Tiffany. The place is beautiful," Alex said.

"Oh, Alex, come on. Malik knows he doesn't need an invitation," I said, while keeping my eyes on Malik. I was glad that I'd allowed my sister to talk me into such an expensive outfit. "How are things at the office, Malik?"

He moved his mouth to say something, but Alex talked right over him. "Did Malik tell you he made partner?" she asked, slipping her arm through his.

"Absolutely! Or at least I do believe that's what he whispered in my ear the other night," I responded, then winked at him.

"Malik, honey, what is she talking about?"

While Malik stood there dumbfounded, mumbling some excuse to Alex, I motioned to one of the waiters. "Bring me a bottle of champagne, make it Cristal." I looked from him to her and said, "Only the best for Malik and his *friend*."

But of course our celebration was cut short when G-dog came up and stood beside me.

"Yeah, what's up? What's all the smiling about over here?" he asked, staring hard at Malik.

Malik's jaw clenched before he spoke. "Good evening, *G-dog*. What's up with you?" he asked, not extending his hand to shake.

I chuckled at the way Malik pronounced his name.

"You can call me Greg, and it's all good, man." He turned from Malik and said to me, "C'mon, Tiffany. I got some people I want you to meet."

G-dog's people turned out to be his Cuban friends from Miami. They looked pretty shady, but that was his life.

Around 9:30 I stepped outside to get a breath of fresh air and also to watch the excitement of the crowd. Both sides of the velvet ropes outside the club were lined with people willing to pay the fifty-dollar cover charge for opening night at Teaz. The valets were parking cars for which they'd run out of spaces. I watched as people feverishly tried to beg or bribe their way past the bouncers into the club. Police barricades lined the sidewalk across the street in front of Rittenhouse Square, where onlookers stood hoping to catch a glimpse of celebrities. The line stretched from the corner of Eighteenth and Walnut all the way to Twentieth Street. Everyone was dressed in stylish attire, no Timberlands, baggy or torn jeans, or sneakers. This was strictly upscale and my security staff was there to enforce it. Of course, the exception was any celebrity who walked through the door.

By 11:00 P.M. the club was packed and people danced shoulder to shoulder. The sights and sounds of Teaz intoxicated even me, and the energy got even higher when Essence took over the turntables at midnight. Her beats and deep sultry voice pulsated through the air. She had the crowd under a spell.

The Sixers' starting five had shown up along with Phoenix Carter, who'd been recently traded to Philadelphia. And players from the Eagles, who everyone hoped were bound for the Super Bowl, were sprinkled throughout the crowd. Eve was in town and she'd even picked up the microphone to rap a few lines, before her entourage took over the upstairs VIP lounge. There were also my special invited guests, who ranged from J-Hova to some of Philly's local celebrities. But I was the one in for a surprise when Leila introduced Pink as a personal friend of hers.

As I pushed my way through the crowd the music seemed to make my body move all at once, like I was floating. I made small talk with those closest to me, nodded and flashed a smile at those I couldn't get to. I'd only had one glass of champagne but the excitement was putting me on my own high. There was no mistaking that the men and women of Philly had come to Teaz decked out in their finest. It resembled an R. Kelly video, like someone had synchronized every move the crowd made. I was the one who had done that.

By the time Outkast came blaring out of the speakers with "I like the way you move," I was certain that Teaz was what Philly club goers had been waiting for and desperately needed. When I tried to make my way off the floor I was pulled back when the crowd started screaming to the sounds of "Hey Ya." As one song blended into another I continued to dance, and I probably would've stayed on the dance floor but I noticed that my friends from Platinum Images had arrived. There were Michael and Kendra, and even Sasha and Trent had made time to join in the grand opening festivities. For them I provided a personal tour of the club, then we shared a toast before I was pulled into an interview for *Essence* magazine.

The party finally wound down around 4:30 A.M., but I was still on a high. It seemed as if I'd met every promoter and supporter from New York to D.C. Luckily, G-dog's people had filed out of the basement around 3:00 so no one noticed that there were two different crowds. Despite the excitement of the opening, my spirits were dampened every time I saw Malik and Alex and how they seemed so into each other. He barely paid me any attention during the evening, so maybe I'd read too much into what he'd said to me the other night. But I refused to allow that to bring me down because Tiffany Johnson was on her way to being Queen of the Night.

10

THUG THURSDAYS

After the opening of Teaz, each day rolled into the next, especially with the flurry of holidays and special events that followed. If all went as planned, it would be New Year's before I caught up with myself. Being in the nightclub business totally turned me into a vampire. I was always the last one to leave. Even though I completely trusted my director of operations to count the money, I wanted to make sure everyone, including the folks in the basement, had cleared out before I locked up. The cleaning people, who didn't come until the morning, had their own key to get in. I'd pretty much gotten my daily life down to a routine. I'd sleep until 11:00 A.M., then head off to the club for a recap and PR meetings, then return home by 3:00 in the afternoon for dinner and a nap before returning to the club at midnight. There was rarely any free time in between.

Teaz was being bombarded with private party requests, most of which came from celebrities, but we also had to honor those who were not. The easiest decision to make was when I received a call from Jada Pinkett-Smith requesting to rent out the club to host her and Will's private New Year's Eve bash.

Teaz also catered to various groups by hosting theme parties. On Thug Thursdays, our most popular theme night, I don't know how we kept the place from exploding. Mix, a local and reputable drug dealer from North Philly, if there was one, had ties to the Cuban boys who were constantly having run-ins with the Jamaicans from Southwest. And then there were the problems with the Puerto Ricans from Eighth Street, who wanted no part of the Italian boys from one end of South Philly. And I definitely didn't want them to cross paths with Black Chalie and Nitty from West Philly. For some reason Teaz had become equal territory. They all respected me and my place of business.

We made money on those nights serving anything that was new. Mojitos, Incredible Hulk, Thug's Gold, Envy, Rushh and Ciroc vodka. And, of course, there was plenty of Cristal. They drank it all and didn't have a problem spending the money.

It was on those Thursdays that I began to see a change in G-dog as he strolled around the club with an unlit weed-filled cigar. I think he thought the place belonged to him. I had to get him under control when I discovered that he'd run up a three-thousand-dollar bar tab. I almost felt like he did it to get my attention, which I hadn't given him much of lately.

Teaz had its share of problems, too. Even with all the security, we were unable to pinpoint the source of all the drugs that were coming in. Ecstasy use was running rampant at Teaz.

One Friday night I'd gone home early to get some much needed rest, but I'd had to return to the club after receiving an urgent call from Leila. An underage girl had passed out in the ladies' room at Teaz and was being rushed to the hospital. The medics were saying that she'd been high on Ecstasy.

I closed the club earlier that night so I could meet with my staff. G-dog passed off the girl's overdose as if it were no big deal and said that his security staff checked all IDs and if it said the person was twenty-one, the club wasn't responsible. His nonchalant attitude unnerved me. I would've liked to talk to Malik, but he'd been so busy being covered by the media and flaunting Alex at political events that he seemed to have little interest left for me or Teaz. There was no way I was about to make a fool of myself.

Essence had been telling me that she'd seen some suspicious activity at the club, but I refused to believe it was any friends of mine. They had too much respect for me. When I asked G-dog about it, he laughed it off and said nothing could get past his security staff.

The one person I knew who had her eye on things was Kamille. I dropped by her house early Monday morning while she was getting ready for work and we chatted about the goings-on at Teaz.

She already knew about the illegal gambling, but she didn't know that I suspected that G-dog was somehow involved with drugs. I explained to her I was suspicious of his monthly runs to Florida. Recently G-dog had even gone to Pinar Del Río, a place in Cuba where he was supposedly involved in a family real estate deal. Kamille began to see my point.

Kamille was certain that I was thinking too small about G-dog selling drugs. She said it was probably bigger than that and brought up a good point: How could he afford his lifestyle on the salary he made working for the Department of Recreation? His security business was too new to be turning a profit, and his family wasn't *that* rich. Kamille believed, and convinced me, that what G-dog was actually doing was running drugs up and down the coast, which brought in much more money. The only thing I was unsure of was whether Mr. Haney was involved in this drug smuggling scheme.

"Why don't you talk to the boy's daddy and tell him what you think?" Kamille said.

I had considered discussing it with Mr. Haney, just to see how he responded. To all appearances, he was a champion to solve Philadelphia's drug problem, so he might not be aware that his son was a drug dealer. On the other hand, common sense and experience told me that this man was no angel. He'd drugged me, so there was a possibility that he was somehow involved in G-dog's drug operation. Until I had more information, I decided against speaking with Mr. Haney. And with everything that was going on, I was certainly not in the mood to fight off his sexual advances.

"I could be wrong, Kamille. I don't want any problems. I

mean, G-dog hasn't been such a bad guy. He just has a big-ass ego."

"Okay, if you don't want to tell his father you think he's selling drugs, here's another plan. Why not join up with one of the antidrug organizations Mr. Haney's part of so you can get closer to him, and maybe he'll have his guys keep a tighter hold on things at Teaz."

My sister had no idea how close I already was to him.

"From the look on your face I can tell you don't want to do that. Is his father that bad? Don't tell me his whoring ass tried to hit on you, 'cause I know you cussed him out."

I wasn't ready to tell my sister about what happened between Mr. Haney and me, so I hurriedly replied, "No! You shouldn't believe all that stuff you read in the paper anyway."

"Alright, but here's my last idea."

"What's that?"

"Why not call Malik? He can talk to Haney about G-dog."

The last thing I wanted was for Malik and Mr. Haney to talk, so I told my sister that I'd pursue her first idea and make an appointment to speak with Mr. Haney about G-dog and the drug problem at Teaz. Maybe I was being naïve, but I didn't want to believe that the DA was a drug dealer like his son. Maybe I was making too much of Mr. Haney's having given me Ecstasy. After all, everyone has a weakness, and using Ecstasy to relax wasn't so bad—for him. I just couldn't let him give that drug to me again. If I had to endure a few advances from Mr. Haney to save Teaz, so be it.

I spoke with his secretary and set up an appointment to

meet him at 2:30 P.M. I felt confident that he wouldn't be able to try anything with me because we were meeting at his office in the middle of the day.

I purposely dressed professionally so as to not make the DA think I'd gone there for any reason except business. His secretary ushered me into his Arch Street office, where I sat waiting for him for over twenty minutes. Looking around, I noticed the shelf of law books, certificates, and commendations on the walls along with a U.S. flag behind his desk and pictures of his family in addition to those of high-ranking city officials, as well as the governor.

Growing impatient at Mr. Haney's tardiness, I was about to leave when he and Joey Colavito walked into the office. He didn't comment but I could see his surprise at my new look. After the introductions were made, which really weren't necessary because Mr. Colavito was a high-profile local attorney closely connected to Philly mob figures, I racked my brain trying to understand the nature of their relationship. The only possibility I could come up with was that one of Joey's clients was probably about to become a government witness.

"I know you're wondering why Joey's here," Mr. Haney began. "But before we get started on our business, we'd like to offer you a piece of prime real estate."

"Real estate? I'm here to talk about the drugs at Teaz."

"Okay, but hear us out. Go 'head, Joey."

I assumed they were talking about the building next door to Teaz, but I wasn't interested in that and I damn sure wasn't about to get in any deeper with the Haneys.

I half-heartedly listened as Colavito droned on about what type of service he could provide for me.

"Ms. Johnson, you could come away a very rich lady if you let us put that building in your name and then sell it for you in a year or so. I'm an excellent lawyer and you would benefit from having me on your team."

"Mr. Colavito, you're wasting your time trying to push that place on me. Anyway, I wasn't aware that you were a mortgage broker. Now, as I was saying, I came here to talk about the Ecstasy problem I'm having at the club."

"That's an easy one. We can just set up a drug sting operation at the club and get rid of those cats. And Joey can take care of all your other business."

"I already have an attorney and really, I don't think a sting would be necessary," I said, wondering what Mr. Haney was up to.

"Ms. Johnson, you can't be serious. Malik Skinner is too consumed with keeping his own firm out of hot water," Colavito chimed in, making me wonder about his knowledge of Malik's business.

"I'm still not interested. Plus, I believe I came to talk to Mr. Haney," I said, hoping Colavito would take the hint that his presence was not needed and leave. He did.

"It's good to see you again, Tiffany. It's been a long time," Mr. Haney said, after closing the door behind Colavito. When he turned around I saw that the crotch of his pants was straining over his swollen penis. He stepped in front of me, his back against the frosted glass door, blocking my exit. Suddenly, I changed my mind about seeking Mr. Haney's help.

"I have to get going. I can see you're not going to be of any help. I guess all that stuff about cleaning up the city is just a bunch of crap you tell your voters," I said, moving toward the door before the meeting got more out of hand.

"Before you leave I want to invite you and my son to the police commissioner's retirement party tomorrow evening. I noticed that my son usually does what you tell him."

"Thank you. I'll tell G-dog about the party, but I won't be able to make it. I have business at the club to attend to," I said, trying to get around him and out the door.

Holding on to the crotch of his pants, he said, "Now, look what you've done to me. You're going to have to take care of this before you leave."

I backed up, almost toppling over an armchair trying to get away from him.

"Mr. Haney, you're a sick man. I'm not sure what you take me for, but I want no part of your sick sex games."

"I think you like the way I fuck you," he said, following me as I made my way around to the other side of his desk.

"You bastard. You think I don't know you put shit in my drink?"

He took that as a joke and practically doubled over in laughter.

"Now, Tiffany, why would I have to do something like that? You practically begged me for it."

"Fuck you, you prick."

He walked back to the door and turned the lock. "Come here, lovely lady, and stop teasing me," he said, placing his hand inside the opening of his boxers.

"Are you crazy?" He had to be to presume that I'd have sex with him in his office.

I was frozen in place, trying to decide what to do. If I screamed, his two assistants were sure to hear me. But what would they do? Would they actually believe that I hadn't wanted it? If I screamed and they did believe me, it would turn into a huge media scandal and everyone would know. Was my only choice to submit to him? I forced back tears, knowing he'd probably enjoy that even more.

"Mr. Haney, please, I can't do this, not here." What was I saying? I couldn't do this with him anywhere, ever again.

"It's nice you're trying to be tough, but you know you want me to fuck that pretty black ass. Now, come on over here."

In the few moments I took to consider my choices, he had his hands all over me. I'd just scrambled out of his grip when someone tapped on the door. He ignored the person at the door and continued his pursuit, until he finally caught me and pushed me over the back of a chair. If it hadn't been for the fact that I was wearing pants he would've gotten what he wanted. As he struggled with my pants I picked up his silver letter opener from his desk. I twisted around and held the blade against his now exposed dick.

"You're only going to make it harder. You know how hard and long it gets for you," he said, stroking himself. "Go ahead, cut me. I won't tell."

I dropped the opener, picked up my things, and ran out of his office. I could hear him laughing behind me.

Riding the elevator down to the lobby, I was disgusted with myself and hating Mr. Haney. I wondered how many women he had at his mercy. I had to get away from him and his son. And as for the drugs at Teaz, I realized that Mr. Haney could not have cared less. I decided then that I wanted to replace G-dog's security company and get the gambling out of Teaz, even if that meant seeking Malik's help. He was, after all, my attorney.

I tried to get out of attending the commissioner's party the following evening, which was being held at a ballroom at the Bellevue, but G-dog insisted it would be good for business. I knew he was right; I needed the city behind me so there wouldn't be any problems for Teaz.

I dressed for the occasion in a short black cocktail dress, and for the first time since I'd known him, G-dog wore a tux, complete with bow tie and black shiny shoes.

G-dog had been right. There were plenty of city officials present, including the mayor, who congratulated me on Teaz and offered whatever assistance he could provide.

I was glad to see Mrs. Haney, whom I'd taken a liking to. I wanted to understand how this well-bred white woman had gotten caught up in a sham of a marriage to a man who cheated on her. If that's where she thought my relationship with G-dog was headed, then she was sadly mistaken.

"Tiffany, I'm so glad you're here. I've been wanting to thank you for encouraging my son to get his life together," his mother commented, as we stood having a drink together at the bar, both watching G-dog interact with the politicians who ran Philadelphia.

I had no idea what she was talking about, and didn't try to hide it. "I don't think I had anything to do with that."

"Surely you did. Prior to your coming into his life he had absolutely no interest in politics. His only interest was his father's money." Her cynical laugh told me that was her only interest, too.

This was the first mention I'd heard of G-dog stepping into the political arena.

"And what about you, Mrs. Haney? What's your interest in politics?" I was hoping the look on my face told her that I wanted to know more about this family.

She looked around the crowded room and said, "Tiffany, we should get together one day, to chat. Outside of one of these functions."

I was about to dig a little deeper but Mr. Haney interrupted me.

"And what could you two possibly be talking about?"

"Your son," she said curtly.

He turned to look at me and asked with pride, "Did my wife tell you that my son has decided to go into politics?"

Oddly, I noticed that Mrs. Haney cringed at her husband's nearness.

"Yes, she did. I'm sure that makes you ecstatic."

Nelson, the retired police commissioner, walked up and joined in the conversation. "Ms. Johnson, how are things going at the famous Teaz nightclub?"

I looked at Mr. Haney before responding. "Everything is going quite well."

"Tiffany, are you sure you don't need any assistance from the commissioner?" Mr. Haney asked, after picking a shrimp from the passing tray of hors d'oeuvres.

"If I do, I'll be sure to let your son know."

Commissioner Nelson put his hand on Mr. Haney's shoulder, smiled at him, then added, "I hear you had some problems down there."

"Unfortunately, some young girl high on Ecstasy managed to use a fake ID and get in the club. But the situation is under control now."

"Well, if there is any more trouble, just let me know and I'll post a few men over there. Just because I'm retiring doesn't mean I don't still have some pull in this town."

"I'm sure you do. But if you'll excuse me, I'd like to go freshen up."

When I walked away I turned my cell phone on so I could check on things at the club. The screen read six messages, and before I could listen to them the phone started to ring. It was Leila.

"Tiffany, you gotta get over here right away. We just had someone OD outside the club. The medics didn't get here in time. The cops are talking about getting a search warrant."

"What?" My voice was loud, causing others who were standing close by to turn around and take notice. "Are you telling me somebody is dead outside the club?"

"Yes, yes, that's what I'm saying. You need to get here right away."

"I'm on my way."

I looked around the ballroom for G-dog but he wasn't in sight. Instead I spotted Mr. Haney across the room flirting with the president of the city council. I made my way to them, and as soon as she walked away, I quickly explained the situation.

Without asking too many questions, Mr. Haney went into action. He strode across the room and found G-dog, and they both huddled with two other city officials plus the commissioner and began to make calls on their cell phones. They were still making calls when I left the party and headed over to Teaz.

It only took me five minutes to drive down Walnut Street to the club. When I pulled up there was so much police activity that, rather than try to get into my reserved space, I pulled up onto the sidewalk. As I was about to get out of my truck, my cell phone rang.

"Hey, lovely lady, I have good news. The warrants have been quashed and you'll be able to reopen in a few days once the investigation is over. Just sit tight and one of my people will be over to talk to you."

"That's it? Just sit and wait?"

"Now, tell me. When are you going to realize that I own this town?"

"Thank you, Mr. Haney," I said, truly appreciative yet knowing that it came with a price.

11

NEW YEAR'S

By New Year's things had settled down. The saving grace was that the person who died hadn't been inside of the club. The good that came out of it was that G-dog moved his gambling out of the basement right after the incident. So that was one tie that had been cut. I'd deal with severing my relationship with G-dog after the New Year's bash we were hosting.

Will and Jada's party was splendid. There were about one thousand attendees. They brought in sponsors from Cohiba cigars and purchased $4,000 bottles of Rémy Louis XIII. Their event took over the entire place, making it a first for a Philly nightclub.

Since it was their event my work was minimal, allowing me

time out to enjoy myself with their celebrity guests and all the compliments I was receiving on Teaz. The night was going great, that is until I saw Malik. Why was he here if everything was over between us? And why did he need to be here at Teaz celebrating his New Year's with Alex? He'd made no other attempts to talk to me and hadn't returned my calls to his office when I'd called seeking his assistance. I refused to let him get under my skin. I had just made up my mind to ignore them when they made their way toward me. I was doing well with our small talk until I noticed the marquise diamond on Alex's left hand.

I turned my attention to Malik so I wouldn't stare at the ring on her finger. "How's life as a partner? Busy, I'm guessing."

Malik stumbled over his words. "Huh, busy. I mean, yeah. It's very busy."

"Has Malik told you our news?" Alex chimed in.

"Now, what would that be, Malik?" I asked, summoning a fake smile.

Alex's bubbly voice answered for him. "Malik has asked me to marry him."

I was crushed. Now I realized why I hadn't heard from him. I'd never known Malik to be a player, but he'd surely played me. The punk hadn't even had the nerve to tell me. But then, maybe that's what he'd been trying to say to me when we'd gone to dinner and again that night when I'd given him a tour of the club.

"That's real nice, Malik. I'm happy for you." I cleared my throat. "When's the big day?"

Again Alex answered for him. "I haven't set a date yet, sometime in the spring."

I wanted to wring her little white neck. G-dog saved me when he walked up behind me and laced his hand through mine. He appeared to be pretty drunk, and from the glassiness of his eyes I could tell he was high on something else.

"What's up, Malik? You still trying to get my girl?" he asked, while his fingers traced up and down my bare arms.

Malik shook his head slowly, and pressed his lips together. I could tell he was thoroughly disgusted and, regardless of the fact that his fiancée stood next to him, it was killing him to see me with G-dog.

"I'm just out ringing in the New Year," Malik said with little emotion.

"Yeah, right. Well, I'm sure I'll be seeing you around. Did Tiffany tell you that I'm working with my father now?"

Malik chuckled and said, "You, in politics? Well, that should prove to be interesting. Anyway, you two have a good night. Tiffany, I'll get you on my schedule for next week."

After they walked away G-dog was full of questions. "What the hell you meeting him for?"

"Business, G-dog. Remember, he is my attorney for the club."

"Ain't like that can't be changed. You sure it wasn't more than that going on?"

"I was congratulating him on his engagement."

G-dog found that hysterical and couldn't seem to stop laughing. "That's good news. Maybe now you'll get over that nigga."

G-dog's comment reaffirmed my decision to end our relationship. I would deal with him soon. I turned away and watched as Malik and Alex pranced around the club enjoying themselves.

While I stood at the bar talking to Leila and Kamille and downed probably my third glass of Moët, my sister picked up that something was wrong.

"You know, it's not too late to get your man back," she said.

"Kamille, you're crazy. Malik doesn't want me. They're engaged."

"Girl, that's all bullshit. That man loves your ghost and you know it. He does not want that skinny bitch."

"You're crazy. A man doesn't get engaged if he's in love with someone else."

"He does if he's trying to make some moves. Wasn't her father head of the Democratic Party or some shit?"

"I don't know. Anyway, it doesn't matter. It's over."

"All I'm saying is it's not too late."

My sister was beginning to piss me off. "It's over between us, Kamille. I told you, he doesn't want me. Now, can you let it go?" How could I push it out of my mind if my sister wouldn't stop talking about it?

"Whatever you say," she added, then walked back over to her date.

It wasn't that I hadn't thought about making one last plea to Malik. If he'd really loved me, then he couldn't want to marry her that bad. But who was I to break up someone's engagement? I stood at the bar talking to Leila, who said she'd be my date for the night, and I almost wished she would. I knew she'd had a little too much to drink, or maybe she was just trying to lift my spirits, because she never flirted with me. None of us usually drank while working, but New Year's Eve was a bit of an exception.

It was getting close to midnight and I planned to be out of sight when the clock struck twelve. There was no way I'd ring in the new year watching Malik kissing Alex.

By 11:40 I figured I'd have one last glass of champagne and slip into my office before anybody noticed. But G-dog stopped me before I could get away and insisted on ordering another round of drinks.

"I'm surprised to see you drinking," he said, reaching down into the low-cut back of my dress. I shook him off.

"I just thought I'd indulge in a little champagne tonight."

"Can I join you?"

"Sure, I don't care."

"Yeah, I been getting the 'don't care' vibe from you for a while now. Looks to me like you're still interested in him," he said, nodding toward Malik, who stood at a table talking with his friend Brad and his wife.

"That's bullshit," I said. "I'm totally over that relationship, and I wish you'd find something else to trip about."

"How about you get interested in this?" he said, kissing me on my back and rubbing his hardness up against me.

"What! What are you doing?" I asked, my drink splashing onto the bar.

"It's been a while. What, damn near two months."

"I've been busy."

"Not with me."

It had been a while. And after hearing Malik's news, maybe I needed something to take my mind off things.

"You telling me you don't miss this?" he asked, grinding his body up against mine while we both watched Malik and Alex move onto the dance floor. I felt G-dog's hand slide up under the short dress I was wearing.

"Get her another drink and make it a double," G-dog called to Leila.

The bar area was too crowded for me to move away from him. There were people behind us and folks standing on both sides of us. I was sure someone would notice that he had his hand under my dress, especially when he began to twist and turn his middle finger inside me.

He whispered in my ear, "Tell me you don't like it."

I didn't answer because I couldn't. I was so surprised by what he'd done I could only stand stiffly in my spot.

"What about this?" he asked, before jamming another finger inside me, pushing them both up even farther.

I sank onto him and didn't care who saw me because my eyes were now focused on Malik, who was dancing with Alex. But now G-dog was working his fingers in and out of me with his thumb pressing down on my clit. I carefully picked up my drink with two hands and gulped it down. I turned my head in search of his lips, but he burst out in that ridiculing laugh, which was a trademark of him and his father's.

"Just look at that square ass nigga. He ain't never made you come like this, did he? That nigga got another bitch now."

"I'm . . ." My voice trembled, which only made him sink his fingers deeper in search of that spot.

I knew I was about to come. I muffled my screams by biting down on the side of my hand. He used his free hand to bend me slightly farther over the bar. With his mouth close to my ear, he laughed, then bit down on my earlobe.

I caught Leila watching me in the mirror behind the bar. I'm sure she was very much aware of the sideshow we were performing. And I could've sworn I saw her smiling at me, too. I could hear DJ Essence on the microphone along with Carson Daly. The plasma screen was showing the ball beginning to drop in Times Square. Across the club everyone began counting: Ten, nine, eight, seven, six . . .

I never knew when twelve o'clock hit because I was coming all over G-dog's fingers.

"Maybe now you know who your man is," he said, then dipped his fingers into his glass of Cristal.

12

IDES OF MARCH

Once the holidays had passed, the club was practically running twenty-four hours a day, with Sunday brunch, happy hours during the week, and of course the infamous Thug Thursdays. Needless to say, the incredible Super Bowl party we'd hosted still had people talking. I'd finally agreed to let Essence and Leila host a Girlz Night Out, which also was proving to be successful.

The only problem that seemed to be on the rise was the drug contraband being found in the bathrooms. The other thing that was cause for concern, which Leila pointed out, was the consumption of bottled water at Teaz. Kamille said it was a sign that large quantities of Ecstasy, which tends to dry up bodily fluids, were being consumed. We were making as much money off bottled water as we were off liquor. When I mentioned it to G-dog he refused to accept the fact that his bouncers were overlooking the use of any drugs at the club. I, on the other hand, believed otherwise.

Needing a break and some time to think, I convinced my sister to ride with me up to the Hamptons so she could assist me in decorating the house. Because of some water damage, it had taken longer than expected for the owners to have the house renovated. It all worked to my advantage since I hadn't had the time to get up there anyway. My parents agreed to watch Kamille's boys and Leila agreed to oversee the operations at the club while we went off for a long weekend. So Kamille, Bruiser, and I jumped in my truck and drove up to the house. Kamille was thrilled to have some freedom and needed a break as much as I did. She had no idea what I was planning to tell her.

Kamille wanted to see the area she'd heard so much about. So we started out early our first morning to look for furniture at antique shops and flea markets. We had lunch at a sidewalk café and then spent three hours shopping at an outlet mall. Kamille's shopping stamina always exhausted me, so on Saturday evening I insisted we flop down in the sparsely furnished living room and share a bottle of Jamaican rum.

"Any luck with the investigator's search for your father?" I asked.

"No, nothing. He keeps running into dead ends. Maybe I should just give up."

"No way I'm letting you do that. You've come too close." I could see she'd lost all her enthusiasm about finding her father.

"Whatever, it doesn't even matter anymore."

"What about the new job? You heard anything?"

"It didn't pan out. But that's okay because I'm pursuing an opening at Mitchell and Titus now. I'm about to go on my second interview with them. It's taking forever."

"Well, be patient. It'll happen. You've got a lot to offer any employer. It's just a matter of time before the right place grabs you up."

I found myself stalling.

"Kamille."

"Yeah?"

"I need to talk to you about something I got myself into."

"What's wrong?"

"Well, actually, it's two things. I mean two people. Separate issues, but they're related."

"Sis, you're talking in circles. Just spit it out."

And I did. First, though, was my concern about the drugs at Teaz and how I was almost positive G-dog was involved because lately he seemed to be high a lot himself.

"So what are you saying? I mean, you've already told me about the drug situation. And I'm guessing you haven't done anything about it since our last discussion."

I shrugged.

"No time like the present, Tiff. We can just make some phone calls and get his ass set up."

"Yeah, right, like I can just call the cops and have him busted."

"That's not what I mean. Why don't you call Malik? He is our attorney, remember. We could start with canceling G-dog's security contract."

"I'm not bringing Malik into this. At least not yet."

"Alright, then. What happened to your talk with Mr. Haney? Surely he can do something. Maybe—"

I stopped her by putting my hand over her mouth.

"Kamille . . ." I hesitated, trying to think of the right way to say it, but then just blurted it out. "I've been fucking Mr. Haney."

For the first time my sister was speechless. I held my breath.

"You really fucked up, Tiffany."

She was totally unsympathetic as I tried to explain myself. "You don't understand. It was a mistake. He came to the club one night—"

"What was he doing at the club?"

"He was bringing the permits I needed to continue construction at the club. We started drinking and doing other stuff and things got out of hand. I was confused."

"I'm sorry, but there's no way you can justify fucking that boy's father. I mean, why were you drinking with him anyway?"

"I don't know. Please, Kamille, try to understand. I'm not perfect. That's why I asked you about the Ecstasy. I took some the first time we got together. And I think he spiked my drink with it another time."

"Tiffany, you may have gotten in too deep. You gotta know that fucking G-dog's father is pretty low."

The way she was looking at me made me wish I'd never told her.

But I needed Kamille to know everything in order to help

me set things right. I explained to her what had happened, both at the club and at my house. I didn't spare any detail. Even though Mr. Haney used drugs to seduce me, I was not totally unwilling. I'd been attracted to him from the first time I saw him on television, and the drugs allowed me to fulfill a fantasy I hadn't really known I had. After I finished speaking, Kamille was silent. Then she shook her head.

"Tiff, you've got to get rid of these Haney men. I wish I'd known earlier about the DA giving you drugs. . . ." Kamille trailed off, leaving me unsure of what she was getting at.

"What do you mean? And how can I get rid of them? Mr. Haney saved Teaz by squashing the investigation into that girl's death outside the club. I'm indebted to him for that. I don't see a way out of this—"

"No doubt, it's going to be hard. From what you've said, Haney seems like a freak, and now I'm sure he's involved with the drug dealing inside of Teaz."

"Kamille, that's a stretch. Haney's using Ecstasy doesn't make him a dealer."

"Tiff, it's just too much of a coincidence that Haney's carrying Ecstasy like breath mints and his son is dealing drugs in our club. You know what? I think Haney's the mastermind behind G-dog's operation. I mean, G-dog's not that smart, and Haney probably gets rid of anyone who tries to point a finger at his boy. Look at the way he made that girl's death disappear. I bet Haney's mission to rid Philadelphia of Ecstasy is probably just him trying to get rid of the competition."

Kamille's reasoning made sense to me and I couldn't

believe I hadn't put all the pieces together before. I leaned forward and hugged my sister. Now that I had Kamille on my side, I knew I could tackle this problem.

After our chat we put away all of the stuff we'd bought for the house, then strolled down to the waterfront to enjoy the beach. That night, I collapsed in bed, drained physically and mentally. I had to find a way to get the Haney men out of my life without making them angry enough to ruin me and my club.

When we returned to Philly the following afternoon I'd only been home for a few hours when a pissed-off G-dog showed up at my door.

"Hi G," I said, not wanting to let him in. "I was going to call you. We need to talk."

"Where the fuck you been all weekend that you couldn't answer your phone?" He pushed past the door, grabbed my ringing cell phone off its charger, and threw it across the living room onto the couch.

His anger was a total surprise to me. I'd seen him jealous before but never to the point where he'd scared me. But as I looked a little closer it was obvious that G-dog was either drunk or high on something.

"G-dog, what the hell is wrong with you?"

"You think I'm stupid," he screamed as he came toward me.

"No, G-dog. But you're out of control right now," I said. I backed away from him until he had me pinned against the wall.

"Like I didn't notice you ain't been around all weekend. Now, where you been, bitch?"

"Look, I've been around, but I've been busy. I have a nightclub to run, remember?" There was no way I was telling him about my house in the Hamptons.

"Don't give me that bullshit! What is it, Tiffany? That nigga decide to take you back? Or now that you got what you want from me, you don't need me anymore?"

"What are you talking about?" I asked, inching away from him and making my way to the couch, where my cell phone had landed.

His breath reeked of alcohol and his face was turning red. He positioned himself in front of me, blocking my ability to move once again. I had to get him out of here. I sat down on the couch and groped for the cell phone.

"Oh, so it's just me, uh? You don't want me?"

"G-dog, it's not that," I said, trying to move him out my way. He shoved his hand into my chest, and I flopped back onto the couch, hitting my head against the wall.

"Look, you need to chill out," I said, rubbing the back of my head.

"You bitch." He squeezed my jaw tight between his hands until tears came to my eyes. "You think you can just use me and my father."

"Use you?" I gasped, and groped for my phone to call for help.

By now Bruiser was jumping against the screen door and barking furiously.

"What I wanna know is where the fuck you been all god-damn weekend," he said, then dropped his hands from my face.

"Keep your hands the fuck off me or I'm going to call the cops, or better yet, maybe I'll call your father," I said, getting up from the couch in search of something to hit him with. I was ready to put up one hell of a fight.

"My father doesn't give a fuck about you and neither do I! You weren't anything but a used-up piece of ass anyway."

I mumbled, "That isn't what your father thought," but in my rage it came out louder than I'd intended.

"What did you say?" he asked, coming up behind me.

I suddenly feared that he might be carrying a gun. Instead of repeating myself I made a fast dash to the kitchen to unlock the back door.

G-dog caught me from behind and grabbed me by my flimsy cotton dress, yanking it up from the bottom. "You really think your black ass is hot shit, don't you?"

"Look, G-dog. I'm not one of them bitches in the street, so don't come at me like that."

Bruiser could no longer wait for me to open the back door. He burst through the screen, scaring G-dog, who backed up into the living room with Bruiser barking and baring his teeth at him.

"Tiffany, you got some shit coming to you, believe me. You, and that fuckin' Malik," he screamed before he backed out the front door.

"Fuck you, G-dog. You're done at Teaz. You hear me?"

Once he was gone I paced the floor trying to decide what to do. After giving Bruiser some water and calming him down, I called my sister but couldn't catch up with her. I only had one option left.

I reached out to Malik.

"Tiffany, hey! I'm sorry to take so long in getting back to you but I've been out of town. Alex and I went down to Clemson."

I didn't need to hear this, but I made an effort to keep my voice neutral. "I see. Well, I'm glad you're back and I hope you raised a lot of money. . . . Malik . . . I have a problem."

"What is it now, Tiffany?" I thought I heard a bit of disgust in his voice. He probably knew it would come to this.

"I need to know how I can force G-dog out of Teaz."

Suddenly he perked up. "That's not going to be easy, not unless you have the money to pay him off."

"Pay him off?" I shouted into the phone.

"Calm down. I don't mean anything illegal. What I mean is you'll have to pay off his contract, and considering all that's happened, I have no idea what other business arrangements you made with him."

"There are no *other* arrangements. Malik, can you get over here? We need to talk this out."

"Give me a little time to figure out some details, then I'll give you a call."

"A call? That's it?"

"Tiffany, there's not a damn thing I can do about this right now."

"Well, while you're figuring things out I'm going to try to meet with Mr. Haney. Goodnight, Malik."

"Whoa, wait a minute, Tiffany. I don't think that's a good idea. I mean, we're dealing with his son. Why not let me see what I can do first?"

"Yeah, alright, but you better hurry."

I reminded myself that Malik was very detail-oriented and liked to think things through before he made a move, but sometimes his style bordered on procrastination and I didn't have that kind of time. There'd already been a death outside of Teaz, and now with G-dog mad at me, I couldn't shake the feeling that he would do something to hurt the club. So I put in a call to Mr. Haney, who only agreed to meet with me if I'd come to his office at 9:30 P.M. two nights later. I planned to talk to him about G-dog's drug dealing as if I didn't suspect that Mr. Haney himself was involved. I hoped that he would see that I was beginning to suspect too much and tell G-dog to stay away before I figured out that he was involved. I just hoped I could keep Mr. Haney's mind on business long enough to get my point across.

13

SURPRISE, SURPRISE

I agonized on how I would handle my meeting with Mr. Haney. Two nights after I talked to Malik, the ringing of my doorbell startled me. Before I could answer the door it became obvious to me by Bruiser's wagging tail that it was Malik.

"I've been trying to reach you."

"Why, what's wrong, Malik?"

"There's a problem down at the club. Everybody's been trying to call you."

"What are you talking about? My phone hasn't rung."

All I could think of was that G-dog and his father had turned the tables on me and that the Feds were probably crawling all over the club to close it down and lock me up.

"Listen, I got a call from Essence and she says you need to get down there right away."

"Malik, please tell me I haven't ruined everything."

When we pulled up to the front of the club there were about ten cop cars outside and all the lights were on inside the building. I was afraid to even get out of the car. Malik insisted that whatever it was, I had his support. Once inside, when I reached the top of the ramp, the colored strobe lights flashed, balloons fell from the ceiling, and about two hundred people yelled "Surprise!"

All I could do was cry when I saw all my friends and family there to celebrate my thirtieth birthday. How had I forgotten my own birthday? Had I been that busy?

After the initial surprise there were hugs and kisses and cake and champagne. Even my brother flew in for the occasion. I nearly panicked when I looked at my watch and saw that it was 11:30 P.M. I was supposed to have been at Mr. Haney's office two hours ago. Slipping into my office, I phoned him to let him know why I hadn't shown up. He tried convincing me that I could come over afterward to have a little tête-à-tête, but I told him it would be impossible for me to get away and that I'd have to reschedule.

When I went back out to the party I ran into Leila, who hadn't been there when I arrived. Her appearance caught me off guard. She was dressed like I'd never seen her before. She looked like a real lady in a dress, heels, makeup, and jewelry.

"Leila, you look beautiful. I've never seen you dressed like a woman. I mean—I'm sorry—but dressed like this."

"Well, it doesn't happen that often."

"No, you look beautiful, Leila."

"It's okay, you're right. I don't dress like this. But I did it for you."

Next thing I knew she was leading me onto the dance floor, where we danced along with everyone else. We were out there for so long that when a slow record came on I almost expected to feel her breasts against mine, but instead, when I closed my eyes for a moment, I found myself being pulled into familiar arms. Instantly I recognized the scent of his cologne and the feel of his beard against my cheek.

"You look happy tonight," Malik whispered in my ear.

"It's been a long time since I felt this way, but I'm actually enjoying myself. This was really a surprise. You had me fooled. By the way, where's Alex?"

As soon as the question was out my mouth I regretted having asked it. Why couldn't I just enjoy this moment with him?

"Woman, now, do you really care?"

"You're right, I don't," I answered, then snuggled my face closer to him. I could tell he was searching for my scent as his lips grazed my neck.

My emotions were a mixture of wanting to be mad at him for being engaged and wanting to settle into his arms for the rest of the night. But how could I be mad when we danced from one record to the next and it felt like all the songs Essence played were just for us? I looked around and saw my sister smiling and nodding at me from across the room.

Later that night after the club had become packed with

our regular crowd, I was finishing up a discussion with Jeff when I ran into Malik and G-dog engaged in what looked like a heated argument. It was not the time to be doing that shit. This was not how I wanted Malik to confront G-dog, but what was I supposed to do? Rather than deal with it I ignored them and walked the other way.

By the time I reached the sound studio, where Essence was giving one of her young protégés explicit instructions on what to play, another sight caught my eye—one I couldn't ignore. Malik was now huddled in a corner talking to Kamille. What the hell was going on?

When I walked up and stood between them, the surprised expressions on their faces told me they were hiding something.

"We have to talk to you."

"What is it?"

They looked at each other as if trying to determine who was going to speak first. I knew whatever it was would destroy my good mood. Malik spoke first.

"You were right about the Ecstasy. We've had it traced back to G-dog, including the E your sister took."

Finally it was confirmed. I didn't need to hear any more. I turned away from them in search of G-dog. Malik came up behind me and put his arms around my waist to keep me from moving.

"Wait, don't confront him tonight. You have to think this out. There could be a backlash if we don't handle it right."

"Fuck that! I paid way more to keep this club open than you can imagine. I'll be damned if we get busted for drugs. Hell, that shit practically killed my sister."

I threw Malik's hand off me and headed across the dance floor. G-dog was at the bar talking to some of his friends. Probably peddling more E, I thought.

"I need to talk to you," I demanded, interrupting his conversation.

"What's up, baby? It's your birthday, aren't you glad I came?" He was clearly drunk as he stood there stroking himself, as if that aided him in his thought process.

I practically dragged him into my office, then pushed him into a chair and closed the door.

"Why the fuck are you selling E in my damn club?"

"What you talking about? Who told you that shit, your square ass boyfriend? What you still believing his shit for? He ain't gonna never take you back."

I didn't let his harsh words stop me. "G-dog, let me see what you got on you right now," I said, pulling open his jacket, where he had the Glock nine stuffed in his waist.

"Bitch, are you crazy? If it wasn't for me and my father, you wouldn't have this fuckin' club."

"Yeah, I'm crazy, crazy for getting mixed up with your ass. I want you out of here right now or I'm calling the cops."

"Shit, you took advantage of every penny I offered your greedy ass. Now, stop talking all that shit."

"You think I'm full of shit? We'll see about that." I picked up the phone and he snatched it from my hand, knocking the entire console to the floor.

"I'll have this place burned to the fuckin' ground if you try to start any trouble with me."

I moved to stand behind my desk, and when he took a moment to look at his ringing cell phone, I pressed the button for security. I'd just changed over to a new security service, so I didn't have to worry about their allegiance.

"What's it gonna be, Tiffany? You wanna see Teaz in ashes or what?"

I never got a chance to answer because Malik came through the door, followed by three bouncers. G-dog tried to grab for his gun but he was too slow, allowing Malik to get in a right hook. His fist landed on the bridge of G-dog's nose, which quickly spurted blood down his white shirt.

G-dog fell against the wall, giving Malik the opportunity to yank the gun from his waist. G-dog tried to go after Malik, but Malik stood firm, pointing the gun at G-dog.

"Move, nigga, and I'll blow your brains out."

G-dog was clearly sober now. Everyone stood motionless, with shocked expressions on their faces, waiting to see what Malik was going to do.

"You keep the hell away from her and this club," Malik said in a menacing tone. "Now, get your punk ass out of here."

"I own this place just as much as you do," G-dog shouted at me, "and I can sell whatever I want wherever I want. My father is the DA. This town is mine." G-dog kept his eyes on the gun Malik still had pointed at him as he tripped over himself exiting the room.

"Yeah, well this club is mine!" I retorted.

"Are you okay? He didn't hurt you, did he?" Malik asked when we were finally alone. He held my face in his hands and his eyes searched for any sign that G-dog had hit me.

"No, I'm fine. Malik, this is all my fault."

"Don't say that. I'm going to take care of this. I swear, Tiffany, you can consider him done."

"Malik, can you please just take me home?"

"Sure. C'mon, let's go."

I didn't have much to say on the ride to my house while Malik talked a lot of legal mumbo jumbo on how he was going to make it his business to get G-dog busted. But we both knew it wouldn't be that easy. We couldn't just go pointing the finger at the district attorney's son without witnesses and hardcore evidence.

When we pulled up in front of the house I was about to ask Malik to come inside but I didn't have to. He used his keys and unlocked the door. Bruiser practically knocked him down licking his face.

"I'm going to take Bruiser for a quick walk," he said. "Keep the door locked."

I locked the door, cut off my cell phone, and turned the house phone ringer off. While he was gone I tried to decide what to do. I'd made a mess of things by getting involved with G-dog. I thought about Malik and how good it had felt to be in his arms. I knew he was engaged, but I still felt like he belonged to me.

Malik found me lying across the bed, trying to think through the mess I'd made of things. When I felt his presence in the room I rose up on my elbows and looked at him.

"I need you, Malik," I told him, surprising even myself with my honesty.

He stood there not moving, surveying the bedroom as if

he hadn't heard me. "What did you say? I don't think I heard you clearly."

"I need you, Malik."

"Come here, woman," he whispered, motioning to me with his forefinger.

I leapt the short distance to him and listened to him murmuring all kinds of things in my ear, which brought streams of tears down my face. I don't even remember when we stepped out of our clothes.

I pulled him over to the bed and we slipped between the sheets. Malik had special places to kiss me that hadn't been kissed in a long time. I'd missed his touch so much. I kissed all of Malik's body, savoring every spot, and he gave me the same in return. How could I have gone so long without him?

Over and over I told him I loved him. When he finally entered me, we fell into a rhythm that was all our own until we lay sweaty and exhausted.

It had to be 2:00 A.M. when I woke up nestled into the crook of Malik's arms, his brown eyes staring down at me. Neither one of us spoke. I moved my body farther under his and he wrapped his legs over mine. I fell back to sleep.

Malik and I stayed in bed until three that afternoon, neither one of us wanting this magical moment to end. We didn't talk about the club, about the Ecstasy, his fiancée, or our past. As long as we had the moment, nothing mattered.

When he couldn't put off leaving any longer, we got out of bed and I fixed him a quick breakfast of a bagel, toasted just like he liked it, and a cup of black coffee with sugar.

"Tiff, baby, I just thought of a loophole to get to the

Haneys. I can't talk about it quite yet. I do need you to tell me what you know about any businesses G-dog and his father might be involved in that you suspect might be illegal."

I finally explained to Malik the arrangements I'd made with G-dog for the basement gambling. The lucky thing was that by having monitors survey every room at the club, I'd caught it all on tape. I told him about G-dog's monthly trips to Florida and all the real estate deals he was involved in. I even mentioned how Mr. Haney and Colavito had offered me the use of the building next door to Teaz. I told him everything with the exception of my sexual liaisons with Mr. Haney.

"You really got yourself into some complicated shit, Tiff."

"There has to be a way to get me out of this."

"Are you sure you're not forgetting anything?"

"No, Malik. I'd tell you."

"Listen, I want you to take some time and really think about this, okay? Think about details that could possibly be incriminating evidence. You'd be surprised at what you might remember."

When he finished eating he came over to my side of the table. "I have a little surprise for you," he said, then went out to retrieve something from his car. When he came back inside I barely noticed the bag he was carrying because he was so obviously pissed about something.

"Did you know that nigga is sitting outside your house?"

Malik rarely used that word, so I knew he was angry. I looked out the living room window and sure enough, G-dog was parked in the lot across the street. I hadn't told anyone that I'd seen him in the exact same spot just before I'd gone away with Kamille. He was clearly turning into a stalker.

"That's not the first time I've seen him there."

"Why didn't you tell me?"

"Malik, you have your own life. I can handle this."

"No. I'm going to handle it. I'll make sure he's behind bars real soon," he said, setting a pink gift bag with pink tissue paper inside down on the table. He saw me looking and I quickly looked away, hiding my smile.

"What are you looking at?"

I shrugged, acting innocent, though I knew his gift was for me.

"I never had an opportunity to give you your birthday present. But I don't know if you really want this. I mean . . ."

"Malik, please stop teasing me."

He passed me the bag and when I pulled out the tissue I saw the box inside held a bottle of the hard-to-find Clive Christian perfume. Maybe he was trying to get me back after all.

"Thank you, Malik, thank you. You didn't have to, but thank you."

"So what do I get for it?"

"Use your imagination," I said, before planting juicy kisses on his lips and all over his face.

"Does that mean we get to go back upstairs?"

Rather than answer him I began pulling him toward the steps, but he resisted.

"Seriously, Tiffany, what I need from you is a little bit of time. I just need you to be patient with me about this whole thing with Alex. Can you do that?"

I'd forgotten all about her and their engagement. If he was bringing it up and asking me to be patient, did he want us to be back together?

"But, Malik, I mean, you got engaged. You . . ."

"Shhh. I'm going to handle this."

"I don't want to lose you again, Malik. I'm sorry I was so stubborn in not listening to you."

"Woman, you have nothing to be sorry about. And we're not going to keep rehashing this, okay?"

"Malik."

His eyes met mine.

"I love you."

"I love you, too, and believe me, I'm coming back."

14

APRIL FOOLS

I'd just gotten home from Boston, where I'd traveled with my parents to celebrate Easter with my brother and to attend one of his preseason games. Young Huli was quickly becoming a celebrity among sports fans. He'd made his mark as a shortstop, and I was sure he'd be playing for a long time to come. But the games were so long that I had a hard time staying interested through nine innings.

Since I hadn't heard from Malik over Easter weekend, I was eager to check my messages to see if he'd called. But the first message I received was from Mr. Haney.

"You may be able to get rid of my son, but you can't send your boyfriend after me. You ought to be glad I didn't hurt his little feelings. You have too much to lose to antagonize me this way."

I dialed Malik's home number to find out what he was talking about. However, Alex, his fiancée, picked up.

"Hello, Alex. Is Malik there?"

"Hello, Tiffany. How are you? Did you get your invitation yet?"

You've got to be joking, I thought, momentarily speechless. Malik told me he was going to handle things with her.

"I need to speak to Malik."

"Hey, woman, what's up?"

"Malik, what the hell did you say to Mr. Haney?"

"I told you I was going to get to him as well as his son. Why are you so upset? Is there something you haven't told me."

"I've told you everything. You think I'm lying? You're the one who's been lying, Malik. What is Alex talking about, some damn invitations?" I hadn't meant to go that far.

"I'll explain that later. Greg Haney was acting cocky, as if he knew something about you that I didn't. Do you have any idea what he's up to?"

"No, no. It's just that, well, you know, he's the DA." My heart pounded. Now I was the one lying, but what else could I do?

"I don't give a damn who he is," Malik said. "Haney isn't the only powerful man in this town, at least not for long."

"What are you talking about, Malik?"

"That I was nominated this morning to run for City Council. But right now I have to go. Alex and I have a fundraiser to attend. I'll call you in the morning."

It was evident that Malik wouldn't be able to handle things; he didn't know the Haney men like I did. Plus, on a personal level, he was playing some sort of game with me, and my emotions couldn't take that. I didn't know what Malik had said to Mr. Haney to make him mad enough to almost tell Malik our secret and threaten the club, but I knew I had to get the upper hand in this situation. Fast. But as much as I, tried, I couldn't think of anything I could hold over Mr. Haney to get him to leave me alone. I didn't have any evidence that G-dog was dealing drugs, so that wouldn't work. And my video surveillance of the casino implicated me in a crime, not his son. While I sat there trying to come up with a plan, I noticed there was a live press conference on TV. Mr. Haney was announcing his campaign to run for mayor.

With this breaking news, I phoned Kamille instead.

"Hey, sis, I'm glad you called," Kamille said. "I came up with a plan while you were in Boston. I think I know how we can get him."

"Kamille, what are you talking about? It's too late. He's running for mayor."

"Think about it, Tiff. That's even better."

"No, seriously, I think once he gets the mayor job he'll back off the club."

"That's a bunch of bullshit and you know it. He's a greedy bastard and if nothing else, he'll get even more into your business so he can get his sadistic freak shit off on you."

"Thanks a lot."

"Look, haven't you ever heard of that saying, 'Keep your friends close, but keep your enemies closer'?"

"Yeah, so what about it?"

"The plan is this: you've gotta go up to your spot in the Hamptons next weekend."

"I do? For what?"

"I want you to invite Mr. Freaky up there."

"Kamille, you're not making sense. It skives me every time I think about him getting close to me again."

Kamille lowered her voice as if someone else could hear us on the phone. I knew she was up to something sneaky.

"Okay, but hear me out. One more time won't hurt you. I mean, if you can fake an orgasm with his Ecstasy-dealing son, then you can surely fake one with him."

What Kamille didn't realize was that there was no faking it with Gregory D. Haney II.

"So what's this plan you've concocted?"

"We're going to tape that creep so we can see exactly what he's up to. Then let's see how wifey would like to watch that movie."

"Kamille, are you out of your mind? I can't do that. I can't tape myself having sex with that man. What if Malik finds out? What if that thing got around town or on the Internet?"

"Sis, would you just shut up and listen?"

"Kamille, I can't—"

"Tiffany, unless you got a better plan, you better hear me out. And anyway, you're going to be the only one with a copy, and once it's over you'll have the satisfaction of burning it. Come on, every woman I know has a tape of herself."

"Yeah, but not with the man who's about to be mayor."

"Do you think he can run a successful campaign in the

midst of a sex scandal, not to mention the drugs? He has to pay for this shit."

"I see your point, but he's not going to let me set up no big ass camcorder and tape him."

"Leave it up to your little sister. Just meet me at my house tomorrow when I get off work."

When I met Kamille at her house the next night, her plan had been seriously compromised. It was unusually quiet in the house at 6:30. The boys were in the basement watching television, and my sister was sitting at the dining-room table with a bottle of Bacardi rum and a pack of Newports.

"Kamille, what's wrong? What are you doing?"

She pointed to a sheet of paper that lay on the table.

The stationery was engraved from the National Adoption Registry. I reached over to pick it up and she stopped me, covering it with her hand.

"Tiffany, this isn't good. It's not good at all."

"You found your father?"

She snatched the paper up and shoved it into my chest. I took it from her hands and read the words. They didn't make any sense, so I read them again. And again and again.

Mother, Christina Wims. Father . . . Gregory D. Haney II.

"Oh, my God. No. Kamille, it's not possible."

I plopped down into the dining room chair. My sister and I just stared mutely at each other. This new development was almost impossible to comprehend.

Kamille leaned her head on the table as she burst into tears.

"Kamille, I'm so sorry," I said, patting her back.

"Why'd I do this, Tiffany? I should've let it go."

"You did the right thing, baby. It just turned out to be the wrong person."

She looked up at me, helpless, her eyes red. "What am I supposed to do now?"

"I assume he doesn't know yet."

"Nobody does—Mommy, Daddy, nobody. I can't face him, Tiff, not after what he's done to you. I don't want any part of him."

"Kamille, stop that right now! If this man is your father, then forget about what's happened between him and me. You don't have to get involved. I can work out my own shit."

She sniffed back her tears and stood up. "No, I owe you this one. Fuck Mr. Haney. Do you think I really want to be his daughter?"

"This is your father, Kamille. The man you've been dying to meet since you were a teenager."

"Sis, if he gave me up once, why would he want anything to do with me now?"

And that's when she explained to me what the investigator had uncovered. Her biological parents had been in their first year of college when they'd conceived Kamille. The Haney family had a very prestigious name even then. However, the Wimses were a white family from Kensington, apparently white trash by the Haneys' standards. The Wimses wouldn't allow their daughter to get an abortion but instead took a payoff from the Haneys to put my sister up for adoption. Not even Mr. Haney knew he was Kamille's father.

We stayed up half the night drinking and discussing our lives, beginning with childhood. I soothed my sister's tears by telling her how happy our parents were when they'd brought her home from the hospital. That she'd been so tiny and white I thought she was a doll. I wasn't even sure if I remembered correctly because I was only a few years older than her, but I knew it was what she needed to hear.

By morning I hadn't been able to convince my sister that I could handle the Haneys on my own. I realized her mind couldn't be changed when she pulled out a cushioned metal box that held a video camera and carefully detailed its operation. I'd had no idea my sister was so technical. It seemed she'd borrowed the equipment from the company that provided electronic surveillance at Teaz. It was actually a miniature camera set inside a digital clock radio and CD player. I was to place it on the mantel over the fireplace. I knew what we were doing was illegal and if things went wrong, I could go to jail. But it was worth the chance.

A week later everything was set. I called Mr. Haney and apologized for all the trouble I had caused with G-dog and Malik and asked if there was any way I could settle things between us. As expected, he said I could make it up to him by meeting with him, so I invited him to my little house in the Hamptons.

15

LADIES' MAN

Mr. Haney arrived promptly at 7:30 for dinner. I greeted him warmly, hanging up his jacket and showing him to the bathroom so he could freshen up after his drive from Philadelphia. Meanwhile, to stall for time, I set the table and poured us two glasses of Cabernet. I mean, how hard could it be to have sex with Mr. Haney and get it all on tape? It wasn't as if I was going to allow him to spike my drink again. This time I'd be in control. I had to be.

He wasn't as anxious as I thought he'd be. I'd fixed a spinach salad, filet mignon, and roasted potatoes. We had a quiet dinner as he told me how much he liked the house and about his run for mayor. He was being quite the gentleman, not anything like the monster I knew him to be. I didn't bring up anything about his son, just listened to him talk about himself. After dessert he presented me with a little blue box that held an eighteen-inch string of cultured pearls with a diamond and platinum clasp.

"Mr. Haney, why'd you do this?"

"You've been good to me, Tiffany. And you deserve something nice."

"This is exceptionally nice."

"Here, let me put it on you," he said, taking the necklace from its cushioned box and draping the pearls around my neck.

He tilted my head to the side to lock the clasp, then kissed me along my neck. I wasn't sure what felt better, the cool pearls on my skin or his kisses.

"Come on, let's go in the other room," I suggested.

"It's been a long time, Tiffany. I've really missed being with you."

I didn't respond. Instead, I watched as Mr. Haney made himself comfortable in the oversized chair beside the fireplace. He removed his shoes and propped his feet up on the footstool, leaning back and listening to the sound of Frank Sinatra on a CD.

"This is good music. How'd you know I liked Old Blue Eyes?"

"I'm sure a man of your stature would like nothing else. Can I get you another glass of wine?"

His eyes passed over my body as he reached his hand out to me. "Why don't you come sit over here?"

I thought how it was almost a pity that here I was setting

him up, because being with him wasn't so bad. I couldn't help wondering what he'd think if he knew he'd fathered Kamille. She did resemble him, with that narrow nose, those high cheekbones, and that straight hair. She was actually more G-dog's sister than she was mine. I wondered if Mr. Haney would offer to pay Kamille off to keep her quiet as his mayoral campaign progressed. I'd promised Kamille that no matter what happened I wouldn't mention anything about the adoption.

"You don't have anything stronger than this?" he asked, holding up his empty wineglass.

"Sure, what do you want? I have some Skyy vodka and some Old Grand Dad."

"Grand Dad will be perfect to ease us into a beautiful night."

I went into the kitchen, got two cognac glasses and the bottle of Grand Dad. Setting them on the end table beside him, I watched carefully as he filled our glasses halfway, then asked me to get some ice. I'd never known him to take ice in his drink before, so I figured it was just a ploy to slip something in my drink. I wasn't falling for it.

"Why don't you get it while I get comfortable?" I suggested.

He laughed that ridiculing laugh of his and said, "You don't really think I'd put something in your drink, do you? Isn't it just possible that you were so drunk the last time we were together that you let out some of the things you've been wanting to experience all along?"

I knew I'd never have done those things with G-dog's

father without the Ecstasy, but I had to admit that the man turned me on even before I'd had a drink or taken a pill.

"Go ahead and get the ice, then I'll tell you what I've planned for you tonight." The way he said it and the feel of his hand when he lightly slapped me on the thigh caused me to briefly forget my purpose for being here.

I went into the kitchen and filled the ice bucket, and when I returned he was still sitting in the same spot. I had mixed feelings about the night. Part of me wanted to hurry up and get this over with. Another part of me figured I might as well enjoy myself while doing it.

"Give me a minute, okay?" I said, then slipped into my bedroom to change into a cobalt blue silk robe I'd brought with me for the occasion.

"That's better," Mr. Haney said when I returned. "Now you look relaxed."

I bent over and gave him a kiss, then sat down cross-legged on the floor between his legs. He began massaging my shoulders so I closed my eyes, knowing that regardless of what happened I would enjoy this last time with him. Maybe a part of me wanted to enjoy this night to force thoughts of Malik and his wedding plans out of my mind.

We sat quietly sipping our drinks, and I was enjoying Mr. Haney's closeness. I turned around, slipped his shirt over his head, and began biting his nipples through his undershirt. His head fell back against the chair in enjoyment, and at the same time I began to experience that familiar feeling of light-headedness. But I disregarded it as the overwhelming desire to have Mr. Haney inside me overpowered me.

"You missed me, didn't you?"

"I missed all of this," I said, moving my hands through the light hair that covered his chest. Had I not noticed this before?

"That's exactly what I thought. Now, how do you want me to make love to you tonight?"

"I'll take whatever you give me. I just want you to make me feel good," I said, my voice slow and my eyes trancelike as I looked up into his face.

"No, lovely lady, tonight I want you to do whatever you want. I wanna see you satisfy all your fantasies," he said, squeezing my breasts together.

I unbuckled his pants, reached inside, and let the head of his dick slip into my mouth. He pushed my hands down between my legs, making me stroke my stiff clitoris.

"Feels good, don't it?"

I couldn't answer, nor did I want to. All I wanted was another two inches of his dick in my mouth. But as I began to ease it farther down my throat, I heard knocking. I thought it was all in my head at first, then I realized that someone was knocking on my front door.

"Don't answer it," I said. "Somebody might see you. I don't know anyone up here." I was worried, scared that someone might catch us together.

"Let me get it for you." He zipped up his pants and stood up, leaving me confused and hungry for him.

When he opened the door I was shocked beyond belief to see that it was Leila. I tried to stand up, but I was not only half-naked but also dizzy.

Holding on to the chair, I stood up and asked, "What . . . what are you doing here, Leila?" My words were thick in my mouth.

"I came to see you, Tiffany. Aren't you happy to see me?"

Shaking my head, dimly noting that my vision was blurred, I saw that she was dressed soft and sensuous, like a woman. She'd even put on lipstick. Leila was wearing a fuchsia wrap dress, fishnet stockings, and a pair of spiked heels that I never thought she'd think about wearing. But her boyishness was still there and it was subtly turning me on as much as it had when I'd first met her.

"Mr. Haney, what's going on?" I asked, looking from him to Leila.

Smiling, he walked up to Leila, put his hand under her dress, and kissed her, their mouths open so I could see their tongues touching.

"You know what's going on. You've been wanting my Leila ever since you met her."

"Leila, what's he talking about? When did you—I mean, how do you know him, like this?"

She came over to where I stood, holding my robe closed against my body.

"That's not important right now," she said, slipping her peppermint-flavored tongue into my mouth.

Leila smiled, then backed away and sat on the couch, crossing her long legs, leaving me standing there with my mouth open, unsure if I wanted her or Mr. Haney. But I couldn't have sex with Leila. Where was my head? Why was I so confused?

My plan had obviously gone wrong. I couldn't get Leila involved. Maybe I should tell them about the camera. Maybe then they would get out, leave me alone. I walked over to the table and picked up my glass of Grand Dad. My mouth had gone dry from Leila's kiss.

Mr. Haney came up behind me and whispered in my ear while his fingers felt the wetness inside me. His voice was barely audible because his tongue was slipping in and out of my ear. "I want you to make love to Leila. You do want her, don't you?"

My breathing was heavy and my heart thudded rapidly against my chest. With my trembling hand I attempted to pour another glass of Grand Dad, but he had to guide me. As he held the glass to my mouth I could smell my pussy on his fingers.

It all seemed so surreal. The feeling of wooziness and how I was trying to grapple with my senses. Why was my skin so hot? I glanced at Leila. I remembered she'd showed up at my birthday party dressed almost like she was tonight.

Mr. Haney took my hand and tried placing it back down his unzipped pants, but I'd already balled my hand in a fist. And then out of nowhere Leila leaned past Mr. Haney and kissed me. I tried to resist, at least somewhere in my mind I tried, but before I knew it I heard Mr. Haney sigh as my hand unfolded and began to massage his hardened dick.

I was sandwiched between the two of them while forced to kiss one, then the other, or maybe we all kissed at once. My hands had somehow found their way to Leila's satiny breasts as hers had found their way to my ass.

As if we'd forgotten Mr. Haney was there, Leila and I became enveloped in each other. I began to remove her clothes. She undid the belt to my robe and let it drop to the floor. I could hear her gasp at the sight of my dark skin.

"I'm going to make such good love to this charcoal body," she said, while her hands fingered the pearls on my neck.

She turned to Mr. Haney, who stood across the room lighting a cigar, and asked, "Can I have her now?"

Leila led me over to the couch while Mr. Haney, now naked, slid down onto the floor. I saw him dip his finger into a coke-filled cellophane bag and sniff it up his nose.

Naked, he stretched out, his dick engorged. Leila, now naked except for her stockings and garter belt, slid down onto his face. I watched his long outstretched dick grow as his tongue got lost inside of her. His dick seemed longer and harder than it had ever been before, and soon I was to find out that it was.

"Tiffany, baby, I want you to get up here and ride this dick real good."

"I can't. I'm too high . . ." I said, my voice hoarse.

He yanked me by the arm, pulling me down to him. "Bitch, I said I want you to ride this dick. Now, get down here."

When I attempted to slowly ease down on top of him he lifted his hips, grabbed me by the waist, and slammed his dick up into the walls of my vagina so hard that I screamed out in pain.

"Yeah, you're ready. Now milk Daddy's dick." And with that he put his hands on my hips and began moving me up and down.

Leila turned around to face me while she covered his mouth with her pussy. I was sure she'd been through this scenario with him before. She leaned over him, picked up the bag of coke, and sprinkled some onto my nipples before dabbing at it with her tongue.

I thought my entire body would explode as Leila rode Mr. Haney's face and I his dick. I could see his finger going in and out of her ass and I wanted some of that, too. Especially when Leila leaned forward and began to kiss me. We rode Mr. Haney for what seemed like forever, our juices splattering against his skin until he exploded inside me hard, like a volcano erupting. When he finally finished, he pushed me backward, where I lay exhausted between his legs.

And that's when Leila climbed on top of me and buried her face between my legs. I had to hold on to the legs of the couch to keep from squirming away from her. Leila slowed down and inserted two fingers into me while she licked my clit. She only paused long enough to snort more of the coke that Mr. Haney gladly fed the both of us. By now I'd come so much I thought there was no more of me left, but even when my juices had dried up she found more. I was screaming out her name in a passion I'd never felt. I couldn't go on like this. I couldn't keep coming for them.

And just when I couldn't take any more, Mr. Haney kneeled on top of my face and began rubbing his dick across my lips until I was able to take all of him in my mouth. Only for a brief moment did I vaguely remember the camera.

Finally, with the three of us numb and exhausted, I began

to drink the Skyy vodka. When Mr. Haney had his fill of getting high, he looked at Leila and asked, "You ready to get your pussy ate?"

"Only by her," she answered, her French-manicured finger pointing at me.

I felt like I was in a movie, some crazy late-night porn, but it was real and it became even more real when Mr. Haney sat up and told Leila to go sit in the chair.

I sat there on the floor shuddering, watching them to see what he would do next. He went to the table and sprinkled something in my drink. He brought it over to me but pulled it back when I reached out for the glass.

"You know what I want you to do, don't you?"

I shook my head. But my mouth was so dry and my throat so numb that I would've done anything to quench my thirst.

"You gonna eat some pussy, right? Isn't that what you wanna do?"

I had to believe that maybe it was what I wanted. Hadn't I often joked with Malik about having a threesome of our own one day? But not like this, not with Leila and Mr. Haney. And not with that camera watching. Or was the camera really all in my mind? Maybe I'd imagined that, too. Maybe I was dreaming that I was making love to Mr. Haney and Leila.

"You ready?" he asked

I looked up at the video camera. I heard Frank Sinatra crooning out "Witchcraft" on the CD and could only hope desperately that the camera was operating.

"I can't move."

"You'll be feeling better in a few minutes, I promise," Leila said, while unsnapping her garter belt.

Roughly, Mr. Haney grabbed me by the back of my neck. "Fuck her, she'll do what I tell her," he said, then pushed me down onto my hands and knees and forced me to crawl like a dog the distance to Leila.

When I tried to protest, he began slapping me hard across the cheeks of my ass. But it wasn't his hands that I felt; he was using something else, a belt maybe. All that did was bring a river of juices from me.

As I crawled to Leila, she inserted her fingers into herself and quickly moved them back and forth so I could see the juices she was creating. My skin was tingling, my breathing rapid, and my body was writhing with passion for her.

"Damn it, Leila, spread your legs wider," Mr. Haney told her.

And she did.

Still I hesitated at putting my mouth against her throbbing pussy. I could smell its moist scent and knew at that moment why men were so drawn to taste this part of a woman's body. There was no denying it, I wanted her.

Squeezing the back of my neck, Mr. Haney shoved my head between Leila's open thighs.

"I said put your tongue in there."

"Shut up, Gregory, and let her take her time," Leila said.

Leila rubbed her hands across my short hair and caressed my face as she talked to me. "You're going to like it, Tiffany. I promise you. You're going to like the taste of me."

Slowly she guided my tongue inside of her as she eased her pussy down onto my mouth.

My lips melted against her vulva. Her pussy was hot and juicy like eating a piece of seedless watermelon. The better it got, the more I heard her moan as I used my fingers and my tongue to keep her coming in my mouth.

"Push that ass out to me, Tiffany. C'mon, you know how to do it."

I held onto Leila's knees as Mr. Haney slapped his dick back and forth across my ass.

"Ahhhh . . . I love this black velvet ass," he said, licking between its crack, preparing it before he slowly and steadily slid his dick inside my ass. My body parts were so sensitive and my skin so crawling with longing that I thought I couldn't take any more pleasure. That's when he pushed a vibrating dildo into my pussy.

"Good girl," he said, "I knew you could take it."

Leila was somewhere in a zone, her hands clamped down on my head, assuring me that I'd satisfied her. But Mr. Haney wasn't through with us.

He pulled out of me and stood up, leaving me to rest my head on Leila's thighs.

"Get the fuck up, Leila!" he shouted, and when she didn't respond, he slapped her across the face.

I'd never seen Leila so meek and mild as she immediately did as she was told. Did Mr. Haney have a spell over both of us?

Dutifully, Leila went to her bag and pulled out a black pouch. I couldn't imagine what was next. When I was told to stand, Leila helped me to my feet. Mr. Haney then came to us, and after kissing us both he pulled two red velvet ropes from the pouch.

So there we were, tied, wrists to wrists, ankles to ankles, our soft and sweaty asses touching. And the last thing I remember was Mr. Haney crouching down under the two of us running his tongue along the length of our matching womanhood. All I could do was pray that there really was a camera watching him.

16

REVENGE

There was no morning or night for me after having been with Mr. Haney and Leila. I had no idea how long I'd been lying on the floor covered by a blanket, with a pillow from the couch under my head.

My limbs hurt at the joints and my skin was tender to my own touch. When I finally made it to a sitting position, I suffered gut-wrenching cramps and wasn't sure if I had diarrhea or needed to vomit. I was seeing double and kept blinking in an effort to search for something to help me get on my feet.

My head throbbed and I fought to stay awake, scared that I might slip into unconsciousness. My sister must have experienced the same sensations when she'd overdosed on Ecstasy, but I couldn't go there. I had to fight my way through this.

How could I ever tell Kamille that I'd failed? I'd fallen victim to my own plan. Maybe I'd just tell my sister that Haney never showed up.

My robe lay in a puddle on the living room floor along with Leila's fishnet stockings. There was the half-filled Cabernet bottle and two empty bottles, one of Skyy vodka and another of Old Grand Dad. A black leather whip on the floor caught my eye and I winced and looked down, remembering, at the marks across my thighs. Two vibrators were on the coffee table.

When I stood up I almost tripped over the red velvet rope still dangling from one of my ankles. I wanted to cry. I was so ashamed of what I had done because I had enjoyed it. Despite my fierce hangover and the aches from the whip Mr. Haney had used on me, I had still enjoyed it.

After listening to two messages from my sister, who threatened to drive up to get me, I worked up the nerve to call her. I refused to answer the barrage of questions she fired at me.

"Tiffany, what's going on? I've been worried sick about you. What happened up there? Is he still there? Are you alright?"

"I don't want to talk about it till I get back. Can you meet me at your house tomorrow after work?"

"Sure, sure. Is there anything else?"

"Yeah. Have Essence meet us there and bring her up to speed on what's going on, okay?"

"Tiffany, he didn't hurt you, did he?"

"We'll talk about it when I get there."

"I love you, sis. I'm sorry."

"I know. I'll see you tomorrow."

I finally cleaned up the house, ignoring as best I could the aches and pains as I moved about. I put the tape and CD player back in its box and placed it at the bottom of my overnight bag. I managed to keep down a granola bar and some orange juice, and after taking a shower I collapsed on an unmade bed.

I was still nauseated most of the four-hour drive back down the turnpike the next day. When I arrived at Kamille's I was exhausted. She and Essence were sitting in the living room waiting for me. Essence, seeing how exhausted I was when I walked through the door, ran to me and enclosed me in her arms. I began shaking as I tried to explain to them what had happened, and Kamille took my overnight bag and removed the tape. When they began to put it in the player I went upstairs to my sister's room to lie down.

"That dirty mothafucker. My poor sister," I heard Kamille say. It sounded like she was crying. "Why'd I do this to her?"

"I'm gonna kill that dirty bitch," I heard Essence yelling from downstairs.

I put my hands over my ears to stop the pitying sounds of their voices. They both ranted for at least twenty minutes and I could hear Essence repeatedly trying to reach Leila, leaving her threatening messages both at home and on her cell phone. Then I heard them coming up the steps.

"Sis, I'm sorry I set you up like that. It was so stupid of me. I didn't realize how sick he was."

"And to think he's your father," Essence said.

"Please, I don't need to be reminded of that."

"But that's more reason to make him pay," Essence told her.

Finally I spoke up. "We can't let him become mayor. We have to stop him."

Kamille began hatching part two of her plan. We would carry through our end of it with Mr. Haney, and we would need Malik's help with G-dog. I was worried about pulling it off, but then I remembered something Sasha had said: "You have to strike to win."

While we waited to put the pieces in place I spent every night with dreams crowded with memories of Mr. Haney, which woke me each morning soaked in perspiration.

Essence, who'd been threatening to have Leila killed, hadn't been able to find her since I'd returned. Leila hadn't been back to the club nor was she at her apartment. It was as if she'd never existed.

I couldn't turn on the television or open the paper without seeing not only Mr. Haney's face but also those of his wife, G-dog, and some white girl he was claiming was his fiancée. I couldn't believe he was engaged. It hadn't been that long ago that he and I were involved. Maybe G-dog had been seeing this white girl all along. Maybe I'd been the one who'd been fooled. Could it have been that G-dog knew I was fucking his father all along? But why would he put up with that? Was pushing drugs at the club bringing that much money? There were too many questions for which I might never have an answer, so I just continued to move forward.

Gradually I began to feel like myself. I finally watched the tape to see what exactly had happened that night in my cottage, and by the end of the video I was confident that it was all worth it. I had something that could ruin Haney's marriage and his career.

I'd been avoiding the slew of messages that had been accumulating for a week after that night with Haney until I finally got up the strength to listen to them.

"Lovely lady, it's me. I hope you enjoyed the time we spent in the Hamptons because Leila and I certainly did. I'm surprised that I haven't heard from you. I hope everything is okay."

There were messages from Malik, concerned that he hadn't heard from me or seen me at the club. I couldn't see why he was so concerned, especially since he was engaged. But I needed him just the same. I phoned his office and spoke with his secretary, who wrote me into his calendar for a meeting.

I hadn't been to Malik's firm in a long time, but as I walked down the hall toward his office, everyone I knew nodded and spoke to me. I wondered if Alex still worked there and what would happen if I ran into her. I was in no mood to hear about her and Malik's wedding plans. I was all about business, and that business was bringing down the Haneys and anybody who got in my way.

"Where've you been, Tiffany?" Malik asked when I entered his office. "I've been trying to reach you. Is everything okay?"

"I've been busy trying to figure some things out. Everything's fine."

"Whatever it is, you know I'm here for you."

"Thanks, Malik."

Malik came from behind his desk and sat in the chair next to me. He put his hand over mine. It was warm and calming. I so badly needed his touch, but even more, I needed his help.

"Tiffany, I've finally devised a plan to get rid of the Haneys and vindicate Covington. Actually, the Haneys have made it easy for me."

"Tell me about it." I wished I could tell him about my plan regarding Mr. Haney, just to be honest with him, but that was impossible. I'd have to make sure he never found out about that.

"You told me last time we talked that G-dog travels to Florida once a month, right? And that sometimes he goes by car, correct?"

I nodded yes.

"Well, I've done some checking and that's where he's getting the drugs. What I need you to do is call him and find out when his next trip is."

"I haven't talked to G-dog in weeks. Won't he wonder why I'm calling?"

"Yes, he will. But if you tell him what he wants to hear, he'll cooperate."

"But, Malik, it doesn't make sense. I can't just . . ."

"Listen to me for once, Tiffany. I want you to call him right now from your cell phone."

I relented and dialed the number. G-dog picked up on the second ring.

"G, uh, hi. It's Tiffany."

"What are you calling me for?"

"I saw you on television today, I mean yesterday, and I was hoping we could get together."

"What's this, a joke? You kicked me out your life weeks ago."

"No, G-dog, I miss you. I understand how you feel, but I admit I was wrong. I was simply tripping on a lot of things that were happening at the time."

"That nigga must've finally told you he didn't want you. And I don't know why you wanted him so bad after he fucked your sister."

I looked at Malik, who nodded at me to go on.

"Malik? Oh, he's not interested in me, and even if he was, I wouldn't take him back. I'm through with him."

"Now, that sounds like something I might wanna hear."

I knew then that I could get him to tell me what I needed to know. I lured him back to me by telling him I'd made a mistake and that he'd been the one who'd been there for me when I was at my lowest point. The gullible old G-dog fell for it hard, and all he wanted to know was how soon he could see me.

Finally, after much back and forth, I asked him if I could get away with him the next time he went down to Florida. He was actually driving down in the morning, returning on Saturday. Naturally I told him that was too soon but asked him to call me when he got back to town so we could spend some time together. I had to hide my laughter as I hung up. He was putty in my hands.

That was just what Malik wanted to hear. According to him, G-dog wouldn't make it past South Carolina.

"What are you going to do, Malik?"

"First let's get something straight," he said, looking deeply into my eyes. "I never told you I didn't want you."

"Malik, it's fine. You don't have to explain," I said, resting my hand on his forearm.

He just shook his head.

As we continued to talk I discovered that Malik's plan was to have G-dog arrested in South Carolina en route back to Philadelphia.

"Believe me, the police down there won't stand for a city boy trafficking drugs through their town."

"But I don't understand why G-dog would take such a chance. Why wouldn't he just get somebody else to make his runs?"

Malik stood up and walked back and forth while he talked. I could only imagine what he might look like in a courtroom.

"That's what the drug game and hustling is all about. The chances you take, the danger, the rush and excitement of beating the system. It's all a big adrenaline rush for dealers' egos, and who have bigger egos than the Haneys?"

"What about Mr. Haney? He'll destroy you, Malik, if you go after his son."

"I doubt that very much, so if that's what he's been holding over your head, you can let it go."

"Let's say your plan works. Then what?"

"Tell me what you know about Joey Colavito and his relationship with the DA."

"Like I told you before, I met him in Mr. Haney's office and he was offering to represent me and the club in my legal affairs. And they brought up my managing that building next door."

"Well, surprise, surprise. Wait till you hear this. 'Cause I damn sure owe Mr. Haney for screwing over Covington and ruining his good name. Covington hasn't been able to come back to work since the allegations. I've been waiting to get that bastard Haney for a long time."

That's when Malik went into a story about Mr. Haney. Before taking office, Haney'd been on some unwritten retainer for the attorneys of a local organized crime family.

"What do you mean? And who would tell you that kind of information?" I asked.

"Tiffany, you can never pay off everybody. That mob organization put Haney in their pocket when they saw him climbing the political ladder. All that shit about being a ladies' man, well who do you think supplies him with the ladies?"

"But how can he represent the mob? It all doesn't make sense."

"It makes plenty of damn sense. The DA's office has the authority to appoint the prosecutors who fight the cases, and if those prosecutors are weak and inexperienced, they can be easily manipulated when put up against the mob's high-powered boys. And with that information, I can take Haney down."

It was all a bit mind-boggling, but from what Malik was telling me and judging from the excitement in his voice, it seemed he wanted to do more than just have G-dog busted— he wanted his father removed from office as well. His vendetta against the Haneys was more serious than mine. But my fear was that if they were truly involved with organized crime, where would that leave us if the Haneys got busted?

17

THE TAKEDOWN

It was the Saturday before Mother's Day when G-dog phoned while traveling on I-85 from Florida. I kept up the pretense of how I wanted to see him and regretted putting him out of my life. I even went as far as having a little phone sex. At that point he was just passing through Atlanta. Two hours later I called him and he'd pulled over at a rest stop to use the bathroom. That's when he told me what I'd been waiting to hear. He was about an hour outside of South Carolina. After hanging up I followed Malik's instructions and called a number in South Carolina to give someone G-dog's whereabouts, including the make, model, and license plate of his Dodge Ram.

Two hours later I received a call from Malik saying that G-dog had been pulled over in a little town in South Carolina for speeding, and during a random search the police had uncovered ten kilos of cocaine in addition to twenty-five thousand tablets of Ecstasy, all stashed in the bed of his truck. I guess Malik's relationship with his alma mater in Clemson, South Carolina, was paying off.

Next it was time for me to put in motion a part of the plan that Malik wasn't aware of. I phoned Mr. Haney, who was more than anxious to see me. With feigned pleasure I began recalling the events of our last night together and how much I'd enjoyed what he'd brought out of me. He agreed to meet me at Teaz that evening before opening.

When he arrived at the club he was surprised to find me and Kamille sitting in a booth. Judging from the smirk on his face, he probably thought he was getting another freak show. Not in his wildest dreams would he have imagined that he was about to meet his own daughter.

"Well, well, what's going on with you two lovely ladies?" he asked in an oily manner.

I didn't answer and instead let Kamille do the talking.

I could tell by my sister's quivering lips that she was nervous. "I don't think we've ever had a conversation, Mr. Haney." She took in a shaky breath and said, "I'm Kamille Johnson. You need to look at this." She took the letter from the adoption registry out of her purse and placed it in his hands. He read it over, looked up at Kamille, and squinted his narrow eyes like he couldn't believe what he was seeing. He frowned, then read it again.

"You're kidding, right?" he finally said.

"This isn't something I'd joke about," Kamille replied somberly. "I've been trying to find you for years, and especially since I learned that my mother, I mean Christina Wims, died."

"If this is some story you've concocted to extort money from me, you're fucking with the wrong man."

Finally I spoke up. "Are you saying you don't remember Christina Wims?"

I could tell he remembered her. The way he examined my sister's facial features, it was obvious that he could see a resemblance.

"And what if I am your father? What do you want from me? I mean, what can I possibly give you now?"

"I'm . . . I'm not sure." Kamille was tongue-tied.

"She wants to know why you gave her up," I said.

"I don't believe this. Christina didn't mean shit to me and now you want me to pay off this girl claiming to be my daughter? What's next, Tiffany? This is extortion."

"So are you saying"—Kamille glanced down and took a breath—"that on June nineteenth, 1975, you didn't father a baby girl?"

Now Mr. Haney was tongue-tied. I could see he wanted to compromise. He looked a little weak and shaky, like he needed a drink. I could tell his mind was racing in an effort to get out of this incredibly odd situation.

"Would you like a drink?" I asked him.

He nodded, and this time I allowed myself the ridiculing laughter. After pouring him a drink at the bar, I crossed the room and handed it to him. He took two gulps, which seemed to reinforce him a bit.

Mr. Haney sat in the booth across from Kamille. He placed both his hands over my sister's shaking fingers. Then he reached up and wiped the tears that were streaming down her face with his hankie. Like a politician, he was now jockeying for position.

"Kamille, listen, I was young, Chrissie was young. Neither of us was ready to start a family. But believe me, I often thought about you and wondered where you'd wound up."

"Didn't you even care enough to try to keep me?"

He shook his head. "I did. I came to see you before they took you from the hospital. I held your tiny and fragile body in my arms, but I realized that my parents were right—Chrissie and I were too young."

"But you had money, you could've kept me, married my mother."

I could see she was getting upset and Mr. Haney was growing impatient because he had no idea where her emotions were headed. I'd promised Kamille that all she had to do was tell me the rest of our plan was off and I would stop right there. I thought that's where it was headed and that we would soon show Haney to the door. But then Mr. Haney said the wrong thing. He offered Kamille money.

She couldn't even respond, just looked over at me. That's when I knew it was time to get things rolling. From where I stood by the booth, I turned and nodded to Essence in her sound studio. The lights went out across the club and the large plasma screen came on. I took a deep breath and placed a hand on my sister's shoulder.

"What's going on here, Tiffany?" a confused Mr. Haney demanded, as he watched himself place those pearls around my neck.

Kamille sat in frozen anticipation while I felt my palms go sweaty and my stomach grow tense.

"You whore, what do you think you're doing? I'm going to kill you," Haney barked as he jumped up from the booth and lunged at me.

Kamille tried to block him, and I pushed my sister out of the way.

He grabbed my wrists in his hands, gripping them so tightly that my fingers began to go numb.

"We're going to chip away at every part of your life until you and your son are finished," I said, keeping my voice strong and calm. There was no going back now, and I was determined to bring this man down, for my sister's sake as well as my own.

"Get your hands off my sister, you freak," Kamille screamed, tears brimming in her eyes.

"Tiffany, you bitch, you liked everything I did to you."

He began frantically picking up chairs and throwing them at the screen. It was now showing Leila entering the house in the Hamptons, putting her tongue first in his mouth and then in mine.

"You should really calm down, Mr. Haney," I said, "and listen to our terms."

He backed away and was breathing heavily, looking up at the screen with a bizarre expression on his face. I prayed he wasn't about to have a heart attack because I'd never be able to explain that away.

"What do you want, Tiffany, and what do *you* want?" he asked, casting a cold stare at Kamille, while ruffling his hands through his sweaty hair.

"What I want is you and your son out of Teaz, and out of my life," I said. "I think that's sufficient to pay for the damage you've caused. As for my sister, she can tell you what she wants."

I wasn't sure what Kamille wanted from him, and if she didn't speak up soon, I was going to talk for her.

"I want to be written into your will. I deserve the same inheritance that your son gets. And I also want the building next door paid for and put in my name."

"This isn't fair," Haney protested, sweat running down his forehead. "None of this is fair. What if I just give you, let's say, about fifty, maybe a hundred thousand?"

She ignored his offer.

"It doesn't look like you were fair to my sister either," Kamille said, as we all looked up at the screen and saw Mr. Haney sprinkle something in my drink.

"And what about that?" he said, pointing to the screen. "What about the tape, how much do you want for that?"

It was my turn to talk.

"I'm sorry, but that's not for sale, that's for safekeeping. And just so you know, you only have until tomorrow morning, Mother's Day, at 8:00 A.M. to get everything Kamille wants in writing and have it couriered to me here at the club."

There was no further negotiating to be done. Mr. Haney walked out of Teaz a broken man.

His papers arrived like clockwork the next morning. On Tuesday around 11:30 A.M. I received a call from Malik, who told me to turn on the television to the local news. I sat there watching Mr. Haney giving a speech in City Council chambers. However, in the midst of his speech, DEA and FBI agents interrupted him. I immediately phoned Kamille and Essence.

By the time the five o'clock news came on, Mr. Haney had been read his rights, his properties had been seized, and items were being confiscated. He was being indicted on numerous felonies and misdemeanors including racketeering and drug possession. He'd also been informed that his son had been arrested for drug trafficking across state lines and was awaiting arraignment in a small county jail in South Carolina.

What we hadn't expected, or at least I hadn't, was that the Department of Recreation warehouses that G-dog managed had also been searched and found to contain crates of emptied fire extinguisher canisters filled with small bricks of cocaine.

Over the next few days there were press conferences from the federal prosecutor and of course the mayor, who'd appointed Haney to his position, claiming there would be a full investigation and that meanwhile an assistant DA would take over Haney's duties. Not surprisingly, the assistant district attorney was one of Malik's fraternity brothers.

The following week, as expected, I received calls from the FBI, DEA, and Mr. Haney's attorneys, all wanting to question me on Greg Haney's involvement at Teaz.

Through all of this I was seriously concerned about Mrs. Haney and how she was faring. I doubted if I would hear from her. Her face never crossed the television screen except in stock photos, and she was never seen coming in and out of any courtrooms. Apparently she had distanced herself from her husband.

For three days I watched the Haneys, first on the local news, then CNN, MSNBC, and Fox as they split the screen and showed Mr. Haney being led from City Council chambers in handcuffs and on the other side G-dog being led to and from a South Carolina county jail wearing an orange jumpsuit. They were a sight to be pitied, but not by me.

I could only imagine who had and hadn't been involved with the Haneys. I listened to the reporters: "Few Democrats are lending their support to Haney and most are not surprised by his conduct. Many are trying to put as much distance between themselves and the scandal as possible. . . ."

18

MOVING ON

Malik had been reassuring me that I wouldn't lose the club, but I wasn't so sure I still wanted it. The funny thing was that because of the cases with the Haneys, Teaz had become even more popular. I couldn't even keep up with the jam-packed crowds. We were now as well known as any other club across the country, Nikki Beach, in Miami; Lotus, in Los Angeles; and Rain, in Vegas. I'd even gotten an offer to have it used in the filming of a movie.

Essence, well, she'd basically taken over running Teaz but was also in the process of opening a recording studio in the city. My sister had accepted a management position at Mitchell and Titus and was in the beginning stages of refurbishing the building next door to Teaz and opening a restaurant there. She planned on naming it The Halfway House Café. She even had a steady boyfriend.

My parents still worried about their children. They'd purchased a condo in Boston to be closer to my brother and keep a watch on him, and believe me, he certainly needed watching. They'd never found out who Kamille's father was.

Malik felt we might be in some danger from some of the Haneys' connections still on the streets. So there was extra security posted at the club, and because Young Huli was in the public eye and had been interviewed during the crackdown, he retained a bodyguard. Malik still hadn't been able to figure out what additional information my sister and I had on the Haneys and I had no intention of ever telling him.

Everyone knew that in just a few years Malik himself would be running for mayor. He and Alex had postponed their wedding, though they were still talking marriage. I'd finally relinquished the notion that there was any hope for Malik and me but would be forever grateful for his help with the Haneys.

After giving my deposition I took a month off to retreat to my house in the Hamptons, which I'd finally decided to purchase. I'd decided to add on a sunroom, do some spring-cleaning, and redecorate. It was kind of eerie at first knowing all that had gone on there, but I told myself that in the end, it had all worked out for the best. My sister had got what she needed from Haney, and I would never have to worry about him being in my life again. And the tape, well, once Mr. Haney was convicted, I planned to destroy it. There was no way that was ever going to get out.

During my second week in the Hamptons I was returning home from the market when I noticed a silver Volvo parked in front of my house. There was no one in the car or on the porch, so I went around to the back, where I found Malik sitting on the steps.

"What are you doing here?"

"I came to ask you something," he said, smoothing his neatly trimmed beard.

"Is something wrong at home?"

"No, not at all," he said, taking one of the bags from my hands.

I unlocked the door, still not sure that everything was okay. Maybe he'd found out about Mr. Haney and me. When we got inside the kitchen I put the bags on the table and began emptying them. As I was moving things around in the cabinet, I heard his question very clearly.

"Tiffany, do you still love me?"

I just stood there behind the pantry door, not sure if I should answer him, or what I was feeling for him.

"Malik, you shouldn't be asking me that. You're planning to get married, aren't you?"

"That I might be, but I can't get married without knowing the truth."

I wanted to tell him the truth, that I still thought about him every day and wondered what our life would've been like.

"Can you stay for dinner?" I asked, stalling.

"Only if you answer my question."

I turned around to face him. "Malik, I can't do that. It's

not right. I mean, what good would it do either of us to have this conversation?"

He walked over and held me by my hands. "You need to tell me how you feel, because I'm not walking out this door or down that aisle until I know for sure."

If there was ever an opportunity for me to be with the man I loved, I told myself, this was it. I'd been pushing away my feelings for him for so long, and with Malik's touch they all came flooding back.

"Are you sure my answer is going to make a difference?" I asked.

"If it's what I want to hear, then I'm marrying the wrong woman."

"Well, then, I suggest you take that damn ring off her finger."

EPILOGUE

TIFFANY

A year later, after a very private and elegant ceremony and a two-week honeymoon in the South Pacific, I realized that marrying Malik was the best thing I could've ever done. I never learned what he'd told Alex and never really cared.

Malik and I moved into our house in the Girard Estates in South Philadelphia. We were the first black family to be welcomed there. Our lives had changed drastically. I'd even stopped drinking with the exception of when Malik and I were alone.

We watched the Haneys' trials from afar. Eventually I heard from Mrs. Haney. She'd been brief and only stated that had it not been for her son, she couldn't have cared less what happened to her husband. I guessed she wouldn't discover that my sister had been written into Mr. Haney's will until he was long gone. Maybe by then she wouldn't even care. There was nothing she could do about it anyway. I mean, he had been in sound mind and body, hadn't he?

The memories, though, of having sex with Mr. Haney always sent a tingle up my spine. Even though it had practically destroyed my life, I'd been given a taste of what really turned me on, especially having been with Leila. Fortunately for Malik, I'd eased some of those techniques into our own sex life.

Was it all worth it? I didn't know. We both went through some big personal changes, but we were stronger for it, and so was our marriage. Malik was once again positioning himself in a run for mayor. I didn't care what office he ran for as long as my position was by his side as a happy and, I hoped, soon-to-be-pregnant wife. And Malik wasn't going to stop with the mayor's office. He'd want to go to Harrisburg and become governor. Whatever his choice, I'd be with him all the way. But already I was getting bored and contemplating a new venture for my own source of excitement.

MALIK

There was no way I could have honestly married Alex. All along I still loved Tiffany. I'd never be able to become mayor of this city while married to a white woman, anyway.

Whatever happened to Tiffany and me was partly my fault, but she was my woman, now my wife, so it was only natural that it be my job to save her from the mess she was in. But Tiffany also saved me. I loved coming home to her, sharing our meals, exercising, and walking Bruiser together around Girard Square. Hell, her popularity and personality would probably help me get elected.

I was positive that more had gone on with the Haneys than I'd been told, but that was all in the past. Or at least that's what I tried to tell myself. I had to, because Tiffany was the only woman I could trust.

I had no idea what she'd done in bed with G-dog that had brought her back to me so sexually alive and uninhibited, but I liked the changes. There would be no more infrequent love-making and no need for me to go elsewhere, especially with the way I allowed her to ravage my body every night and she allowed me to do things to her that I never even dreamed of doing. But if that's what it took to satisfy my wife and to make a baby, then she could have all the children she wanted.

The only thing I wasn't so comfortable with was her hinting around that she wanted to start a new business, so I just engaged her in conversation about how many kids we wanted to have, and that took her mind off any business ventures, at least temporarily.

As for heading up the city of Philadelphia, I guess I finally realized that it's impossible to exist and move up in this town as a politician and not have a little dirt under your nails. I just didn't plan on getting mine as dirty as the Haneys'.

MR. GREGORY D. HANEY II

I kept retracing the chain of events to try to understand how I wound up in a federal penitentiary. I mean, I had connections, I was on payrolls, and I should never have gotten caught in this kind of sting. Every time I went into that crowded courtroom I was shunned by the same city officials I'd taken care of. This was not supposed to happen to a Haney man.

My son G-dog detested me. He was doing hard time on a prison work gang somewhere deep in Ridgeville, South Carolina. And my wife never even visited, except when I'd had no choice but to authorize my holdings to her. For all I knew, she'd picked up some young lover and was out spending my money.

Tiffany, I knew, had been part of my destruction. I could've paid someone to take her out, but she still had too much dirt on me that, if revealed, would close the door to that glimmer of hope that I'd get out of here in a few years.

Lying back on my bunk, it was easy for me to conjure up the taste of Tiffany's sweet-smelling body, which had made both my son and me weak for her, so much so that for the first time I'd slipped up. Even Leila had fallen for her.

But every night before the lights went out, I vowed that one day Tiffany Johnson would pay for what she'd done to me.

UP CLOSE AND PERSONAL
WITH THE AUTHOR

WHERE DID YOU GET THE IDEA FOR *THE VELVET ROPE*?

Over the last two years the city of Philly has seen an onslaught of nightclubs, lounges, and chic restaurants, and has been named on occasion the next best place to New York City to hang out. I was curious as to what it took to open a trendy spot, and as I watched a friend venture into the business I decided to create a story that would take people into the world of a nightclub owner.

TIFFANY IS INVOLVED WITH THREE MEN DURING THE STORY. WHY CAN'T SHE BE SATISFIED WITH JUST ONE MAN?

Can any of us? Tiffany thought she was content with Malik, but he left her unsatisfied. They were both more focused on their professional careers than their relationship, so when Tiffany discovered Malik's betrayal it was easy for her to move on to other men in search of companionship and sex. G-dog took her mind off Malik by introducing her to the rougher crowds in the club scene. Though she didn't know it at first, G-dog was using her loneliness to gain entry into her club so that he could conduct some illegal business of his own. As for Mr. Haney, Tiffany had always been attracted to him. He was a successful older man with no sexual inhibitions and he introduced Tiffany to sexual experiences she would never have had in her relationship with Malik.

HOW IS TIFFANY DIFFERENT FROM SASHA BORIANNI, THE PROTAGONIST OF YOUR PREVIOUS NOVEL, *FOUR-PLAY*?

Wow, big difference! Sasha was more mature and confident and knew how to handle men. I think of Tiffany as a younger version of Sasha, before Sasha got polished. Tiffany was insecure about herself and sexually inexperienced, so when she got caught up in a dangerous liaison with the Haney men, she was unable to handle the drama that came with it.

WHICH CHARACTER DO YOU IDENTIFY WITH MOST, TIFFANY OR SASHA?

Definitely Sasha. She's bold and able to multitask when it comes to men. I think my being the youngest in a family of mostly men taught me to deal with relationships with more consideration for a man's perspective, the same way Sasha does because she was raised by her father. But I can also see traces of my younger self in Tiffany. You know, not thinking things through and falling into self-destructive patterns until I got kicked around enough to know it was time to pull myself together.

TIFFANY AND HER SIBLINGS ARE ADOPTED, BUT KAMILLE IS THE ONLY ONE WHO SEARCHES FOR HER BIRTH PARENTS. WHY?

Tiffany sees no need to search for her birth parents because she's satisfied with the life she has. Or rather, that's what she thinks until she discovers the secret between Malik and Kamille. As the middle child in their family, Kamille wasn't sure where she fit in between her successful sister and her sought-after brother. Kamille's search for her parents was the best way for her to find herself.

AT THE END OF *THE VELVET ROPE,* GREGORY HANEY IS IN JAIL. WHY DOES THE NOVEL END WITH HIM VOWING TO TAKE REVENGE ON TIFFANY?

I wanted to leave open the possibility of Mr. Haney coming back to get revenge. Also, Tiffany still thinks about Mr. Haney and their sexual encounters, which is not a good thing considering she's married to a rising politician. Tiffany's got a lot more to lose if Mr. Haney comes back into her life again.

Good books are like shoes...
You can never have too many.

American Girls About Town
Lauren Weisberger, Jennifer Weiner, Adriana Trigiani, and more!
Get ready to paint the town red, white, and blue!

Luscious Lemon
Heather Swain
In life, there's always a twist!

Why Not?
Shari Low
She should have looked before she leapt.

Don't Even Think About It
Lauren Henderson
Three's company... Four's a crowd.

Hit Reply
Rocki St. Claire
What's more exciting than an I.M. from the guy who got away...

Too Good to Be True
Sheila O'Flanagan
Sometimes all love needs is a wing and a prayer.

In One Year and Out the Other
Cara Lockwood, Pamela Redmond Satran, and more!
Out with the old, in with the new, and on with the party!

Do You Come Here Often?
Alexandra Potter
Welcome back to Singleville: Population 1

The Velvet Rope
Brenda L. Thomas
Life is a party. But be careful who you invite...

Great storytelling just got a new address.

downtOwn press

11656